Even the

A NOVEL

Darkness

Even the Darkness

A NOVEL

John Thomas Tuft

A JAN DENNIS BOOK

THOMAS NELSON PUBLISHERS
Nashville • Atlanta • London • Vancouver

Published in Nashville, Tennessee, by Thomas Nelson, Inc., Publishers, and distributed in Canada by Word Communications, Ltd., Richmond, British Columbia.

Scripture quotations are from the NEW KING JAMES VERSION of the Bible, Copyright © 1979, 1980, 1982, Thomas Nelson, Inc., Publishers.

Library of Congress Cataloging-in-Publication Data

Tuft, John Thomas.
    Even the darkness / by John Thomas Tuft.
        p.   cm.
    "A Jan Dennis book."
    ISBN 0-7852-8226-2 (pbk.)
    1. City and town life—United States—Fiction. 2. Clergy—United States—Fiction. I. Title.
PS3570.U377E9   1994
813'.54—dc20
                                                    94–780
                                                    CIP

Published in the United States of America

1 2 3 4 5 6 — 99 98 97 96 95 94

For Barbara

who has always wanted me to write a book about love
and waited until I learned how

Likewise the Spirit also helps in our weaknesses. For we do not know what we should pray for as we ought, but the Spirit Himself makes intercession for us with groanings that cannot be uttered.

Romans 8:26

Prologue

1968

I lay in the dark, holding on to the one pinpoint of light from a hopelessly bleak day. It felt like midnight, as the surrounding woods stirred with the rustlings and nervous twitters of the creatures of the night. Lights-out came at 10:30, and it usually took an hour or so for my cabinmates to fire their last shots of scorn in the direction of my corner bunk.

The ray of light was a beautiful creature named Sheree, the prettiest of all the girls at Camp Fairfield that summer. I was fourteen and she must have been fifteen by my reckoning. And I, Scott Daniels, of all people on this earth, actually talked to her during swimming time earlier in the day.

There I sat, pudgy belly hanging over my wet trunks, when she walked by with a couple of other girls. I'd been watching her while trying to look like I wasn't. My eyes bugged out when she slowed down and let the other girls go on. I gave my knees a good hard stare to avoid looking at the clinging front of her suit.

"Hi! You're Scott, aren't you?"

Good grief, she knows my name. Let me die right now.

"Excuse me, I said hi."

Now what? I could feel her eyes on me, which didn't help the burning feeling in my face and neck. Finally I chanced a glance upward. Her eyes were beautiful blue, and golden hair framed her soft, tanned face. Her smile was open and friendly. I tried to speak but succeeded only in emitting a squeak. To my everlasting relief, her smile didn't change.

"I knew your sister when she was here last year. She told me what you looked like and that you were coming this year, too. I've been looking for her all week. Didn't she come?" Her voice was cool water running over smooth rocks.

"Yeah," I managed, groaning inside at how young I sounded.

"Yeah, she's here? You look like her, you know. How come I haven't seen her?"

"No. I mean, yeah, I'm Scott. My sister couldn't come this year. I'm here by myself." Which technically wasn't true. There were 125 campers for the week. But my gut told me I was alone. And besides, who wants to look like their sister?

I stood up, wiping sweaty palms on my soggy trunks. *Here was a spark of light, here was a goddess, here was the opportunity for redemption of the whole sorry week.* Once I stood, it became readily apparent to me that my knees were in no condition for such foolhardiness, and my voice confirmed it.

"Wh-wha-what's." I stopped, took a deep breath and tried again. No turning back now. "What's your name?"

"Oh, I'm sorry." She giggled, and even had the decency to get a little embarrassed. "I'm Sheree." She thrust her hand toward me.

I let my eyes wander from her face down to the hand she held out to me. It was soft, cool to the touch, and strong.

"You know, tomorrow is carnival night. Are you going?" I was concentrating on her hand and missed the question. "Scott, are you going?"

I quickly dropped her hand. "I guess so." *She couldn't mean . . . could she?*

"Do you want to go together?" I couldn't believe my ears. Things like this weren't supposed to happen to me.

"Yeah. Thanks." And she was gone.

Curled up in my bunk that night I whispered the words all over again, replaying the whole scene a hundred times until I drifted off.

The next thing I knew, I awakened with a roaring in my head. I put my hands to my ears and discovered mushy shaving cream. As soon as I sat up in bed, dirty underwear and jeering catcalls rained down on my head.

"Hey, Preacher Boy! Wake up, you nerd. What's the

matter? Did we interrupt your sweet dreams?" Eddie "the menace" Johnson mocked me in his nasal, whining voice. He was the same height as me, but thin as a rail, with thick horn-rimmed glasses and a large mole on one cheek that sprouted long, soft fuzz.

I had arrived at camp nervous and uncertain. My sister Sue, fourteen months older, was supposed to have been here with me this week, but the mumps put an end to that. My parents insisted I still go; it would be good for me, they said.

Shouldering a duffel bag, a sleeping bag, a blanket with a Bible rolled up inside, and an old cardboard suitcase, I stumbled across the huge recreation field that formed a plateau on top of one of the Laurel Mountains and down the path through the woods to cabin 11-C. Walking through the doorway, the first person I saw was Eddie Johnson. I couldn't believe my good luck. Although it seemed like another lifetime ago now, in sixth grade Eddie and I had been friends, fellow outcasts in Mrs. Frankewitz's classroom. I cheered up, thinking I would have a friend here after all.

Eddie soon set me straight. While I was remembering "Pin the Tail on the Donkey" at his tenth birthday party, he apparently saw a chance to rise above his limitations.

"Hey, look everybody. The Reverend Mister Daniels is here." I stopped short, the blanket tumbling out of my grasp and spilling its contents on the wooden floor.

"Lookee here. What'd I tell you?" Eddie continued. "You gonna preach us a sermon, huh, Reverend?"

By now the whole cabin had gathered around. Eddie was enjoying center stage immensely.

"He's a PK. You know, a preacher's kid. Don't forget to say your prayers tonight, Scottie, or Daddy might get mad and send you to hell."

I could feel the tears stinging my eyes but steeled myself against them. All I needed was to have "crybaby" added to Eddie's list. I had my Bible because it was church camp. From that point on, though, all the boys in the cabin called me PK.

With the other guys gathered around his bunk as he

handed out candy bars to each of them, Eddie would start into his latest plan to raid the girls' cabins or put the counselor's bunk out in the pond. The plans never came to pass, but nobody seemed to notice that or challenge him about it.

Before long he would stop, pointedly look over at me sitting alone on my bunk in the far corner, and then whisper loud enough for me to hear, "Don't tell the PK. He'll go blabbing to the Old Geek." The Old Geek was Mr. Henley, a junior high school teacher working as a boys' counselor for the summer. "Besides, he wouldn't know what to do with panties anyway." This was met with uproarious laughter, backslapping all around, and furtive glances in my direction as they all lowered their voices to murmurs.

When the lights went out at night, Eddie's singsong voice would taunt me out of the darkness. "Did you say your prayers, PK? What's the matter, you too good for us? Why don't you say something?"

I don't want my quaking voice to betray me, that's why.

"What are you doing over there, PK, dreaming of She-ree?" That set the cabin howling. I only got madder at myself because I didn't have guts enough to run across the bare boards and kick Eddie in the mouth.

Thursday morning things took a turn for the worse, if that was possible. An hour of Bible study followed breakfast each morning, and then there was another hour of listening to the camp director passionately trying to save our souls. I got to the outdoor chapel before I realized I didn't have my Bible. Most of the boys didn't bring one, but the weight of it in my hand had become my only link with refuge this week, which surprised me because usually I avoided any outward display of being "religious." Being labeled a PK was bad enough.

I ran through the dew-laden grass and down the path, puffing for breath as I threw open the screen door of 11-C. A movement from one corner of the room caught my eye. Somebody slammed a suitcase lid and spun around.

It was Eddie. The fear on his white face instantly changed

to hatred as he recognized me. He tried to slip something behind his back, but his hand bumped the wall and I heard a soft thump.

I took another step into the room so I could see what it was. On the floor lay a brown wallet with some bills showing. Eddie had been rifling Old Geek's suitcase.

We stared at each other for an eternity. I could feel my arms going numb while my chest continued to heave. Eddie's hairy mole twitched. I outweighed him by a good twenty pounds, but I was the one rooted by fear to where I stood. Eddie knew it. I could see it in his eyes.

"Shut up, Daniels." It was a menacing hiss. "You didn't see anything, now did you?" I numbly shook my head.

"That's what I thought. Now be a good little boy and get out of here fast."

Panic-stricken, I turned and fled back through the grass of the rec field. By the time I reached the tiered benches on the side of the hill, my tennis shoes weighed a ton from all the moisture and grass clippings they had picked up. Some time afterward I sensed somebody slipping into the wooden bleacher seat behind me. I didn't dare turn around. Since only two of us were late, I knew who it was, and I also knew that I would never do anything about what he was or pretended to be.

The rest of the day, through volleyball, softball, and swimming periods, I avoided even looking at Eddie. He was his usual jolly self, rallying his troops around him at every opportunity. At swimming time they all went to the deep end to do cannonballs while I splashed around in the shallows with the other nonswimmers.

I lay on my towel sunbathing when a shadow fell across my face and chest. I sat up with a start.

"Scott, it's me." I kept my eyes down, not wanting to reveal my fear.

"Why are you so jumpy?" It was Sheree's cool voice.

Giving a small laugh, I brushed it off. "I must have been half asleep."

"Well don't forget. We're going to the carnival tonight. Okay?" Her smile made me feel warm all the way through.

"Yeah, I didn't forget." I watched her walk away, letting myself begin to relax and savor the view. Maybe there was hope for me after all.

That evening we met at the bell mounted on a pole outside the dining hall. She wore a pink blouse and white shorts. I pinched myself to make sure this was for real.

As we strolled down the dirt road between the girls' cabins, she chattered away about the water balloon toss her cabin had rigged for the carnival. I was mesmerized, watching her hair bounce against her shoulders.

"Scott, are you listening to me?"

I would kill for that voice.

She laughed at my awkward smile. "What are you thinking about?"

"Oh, I don't know. Nothing, I guess." We stopped walking. She reached out and lightly held my hand. I, on the other hand, held my breath.

She is so incredibly beautiful.

"Sherrreee! Oh Sherrreee!" a voice sang out from the doorway of the nearest cabin. It was one of the college guys who worked at the camp for the summer.

"Jay! I didn't know you worked here this year!" The delight in her voice made my stomach feel like a cold, bottomless pit as my excitement sank to my toes.

Other voices joined in from behind the door, mixed with laughing. "Sheree! Hey, Sheree, come on in. We have a real carnival for you."

Sheree laughed too. "Jay, who else is here? I can't believe it! Scott, these are guys from my home church." My hand forgotten, she ran over and gave tall, muscular, shirtless Jay a hug.

I stood there nervously kicking at the stones on the road, hands shoved deep into my pockets. Sheree disappeared into the cabin. I took a tentative step toward the door, stopped, then turned and walked back the way we had come.

Dusk was beginning to darken the woods as I headed back to my cabin, sure that it really had been too good to be true. Head down, I didn't notice at first that 11-C was completely dark and quiet. When I reached the door I heard soft scurrying sounds. Probably mice checking out Eddie's cache of candy, I figured.

As soon as I was through the door the lights flashed on. Blinded, I squeezed my eyes shut.

"Get him!" With a shrill battle cry my cabinmates descended on me, yanking my hands away from my eyes. "Take him outside." It was Eddie's voice.

The shock quickly wore off. I started to struggle violently, thrashing and kicking wildly in an attempt to break free. There were too many hands. Soon I was hyperventilating and could not scream.

The hands dragged me back through the door, out into the trees. I heard my shirt rip as they clawed it off. Just as my eyes were adjusting to the dimness, somebody pulled a strip of cloth tight around my eyes.

I stopped struggling, confused. What were they going to do?

"Get the towels," came Eddie's voice again.

"What are you doing?" I finally managed to find my voice. "What are you doing? Eddie? Let me go. Eddie, please."

The answer was a sharp crack like a rifle shot beside my left ear, so close I could feel the air move. I flinched and backed away from the sound.

"Everybody got one? Good, now let him have it." Eddie's voice sounded like he could barely suppress his excitement. No one else uttered a word.

There was a silent pause, an awful moment of black stillness. I started to shake uncontrollably.

"I said, let him have it." There was no mistaking the rage in Eddie's voice.

I could hear leaves rustling under their feet, and then the first blow landed. There was a loud smack and simultaneously a sharp stinging like a hundred bee stings at the small of my back. *Wet towels*, I realized, but there was no time for a second thought.

Blow after stinging blow landed on my skin. The night air was filled with the sound of firecrackers as the torment went on. I tried to back away, anticipating the next blow, but I was surrounded. My skin was on fire as the soaked towel tips flicked across the surface. The blindfold was drenched with my sweat. I could hear their grunts of exertion as they labored. Too afraid of what would happen if I fell, I kept my feet spread wide, shuffling in an awkward dance.

I could feel the welts rising on my legs, arms, chest, back, and face. All I could think about was plunging into icy water to quench the raging fire of my skin. "Please, God, make it stop." My voice sounded odd. I didn't know if I had spoken aloud. The words echoed in my head, mixed with the sharp reports all around me.

"Shh. Somebody's coming." The whipping suddenly stopped. At last realizing that my hands had been free the whole time, I tore off the blindfold. I couldn't make out their faces in the dusky gloom.

"Daniels." A whisper from behind me. Turning, I saw Eddie. There was a blur of motion as his towel whipped out from his arm. The blow caught me between the legs. With a low groan I sank to the ground while my tormentors scattered in all direction.

After a moment I forced myself upright. Without thinking, I started back up toward the field, every step agony, my humiliation complete. I was determined not to cry, although I longed to throw myself on the ground and sob until I dissolved into emptiness.

I walked on, away from the lights of the carnival still going on, laughter filtering up the hill. I quickened my step until I reached the doors of the chapel on the far side of the field. It was made of dark wood with a steeply pitched oak-shingled roof. The doors were massive, tall and heavy. I knew it was always kept unlocked.

Before entering, I threw myself down on the grass. The

dew soothed my screaming skin while I stared at the stars beginning to appear high above me. "Why?" I whispered to them. They winked in reply and continued their lazy rise in the sky.

I pulled myself up and went over to the doors. At first they wouldn't budge. Gritting my teeth, I grabbed the handle again and tugged with weary arms. Slowly, with a loud groan, it swung open. I grabbed the other one and pulled it open as well with an eerie screech.

My tennis shoes squeaked on the concrete floor. I stopped to pull them off. The surface was cool and smooth. At the front of the high-ceilinged room was a huge picture window that stretched from floor to ceiling. It looked out over the valleys and ridges of the Laurel Highlands, fast disappearing in the oncoming night. When I reached the front bench I sat down, staring at the giant window, trying not to think about anything at all.

As the night deepened, I started to shiver. Looking around, I could find no cover. Going back to the cabin was out of the question. Finally, deciding it was better than freezing to death, I went up to the communion table. It was draped in a heavy, dark green felt cloth with a gold fringe around the edges. I tugged it off and dragged it back to the pew.

The cloth smelled of mold and decay. I didn't care; it was cover. I curled up on the hard bench and pulled it over me. Exhausted, I slept.

When I awakened, the air was a translucent gray. Beyond the window were dark clouds which prevented me from being able to tell the hour. I sat up, groaning as the pain of cramped muscles and tender skin brought me fully awake.

The clouds fascinated me. Draping the communion cover over my shoulders, I approached the looming window for a closer look. Stretching below me and far into the distance were the dips and swells of wooded hills and shadowed valleys. On the horizon a storm was brewing, its menacing black clouds gathering force.

I watched, transfixed, as a gray-white curtain, a wall of

rain and mist, enveloped the farthest hill. The distant fire tower disappeared behind the mysterious, swirling facade as thunder sounded across the hills.

I waited in awe as the gray mass conquered each hilltop and charged each valley, coming ever closer. Soon I had my face pressed against the glass, standing on tiptoe, straining to catch a glimpse as the advance scouts of mist inexorably encircled yet another tree-covered slope, coming ever nearer. The hair on the back of my neck stood on end as a tingling raced down my spine.

"Scott?" I spun around so fast the cloth slipped from my shoulders. Sheree gasped. "Scott, what happened?"

I hurriedly stooped down to retrieve my cape, angry and embarrassed. When I looked up, she was on the platform too, looking worried as she studied my arms and face, her hands outstretched to help me.

"No."

Sheree stopped, uncertainty crossing her face. "Scott, I'm sorry. Let me explain." She stared at me, her blue eyes threatening to melt my fears.

"No." I shook my head. "No, please leave me alone."

"What happened to you, Scott? It looks like you have bruises all over your body." There was that cool stream again. During the night, however, something inside me had hardened, closed up, and I wouldn't let her coolness reach me.

"Nothing." I pulled the musty cloth over my arms. "Nothing happened. Please leave me alone."

Unexpectedly, a tear ran down her cheek. A big hollow space swelled inside my chest, then threatened to cave inward.

"Go!" My shout startled me. A look of pain came into her eyes. "Please," I pleaded. "Leave me alone."

She hesitated. "Everybody has been looking for you, Scott. I've really been worried. I didn't mean to hurt you. Please believe me."

I was confused, uncertain, unable to withstand the emptiness that now threatened to overwhelm me. *Why would she even bother?* No words would come. Finally I turned and leaned my forehead against the windowpane. Rain pelted it now, little rivers running down against the gray landscape beyond.

I wanted her to stay. I wanted her to leave. She had come to find me. But even as I turned back around I heard the groaning of the great doors as Sheree pushed them open and walked out into the rain.

Thunder crashed, splitting the sky into a million fragments. The force of the shock wave turned the doors back on their hinges and they slowly creaked shut, leaving me alone.

ONE

I didn't know that I could scream so loud. The dream was back, that much I knew. One minute I was sitting in my favorite chair in the family room listening to Gordon Lightfoot singing mournfully about the wreck of the Edmund Fitzgerald, and the next I was lying in a pitch black room. To my left rose a set of windows reaching from floor to ceiling. As I watched them, they swung outward of their own accord. Beyond them swirled a white mist, dense, billowing toward the opening.

The windows rocked slightly as though a strong breeze was passing through. Cold fear filled me as I felt my body growing heavier and heavier. The mist grew brighter, until it was so intense that I had to squint my eyes. Somewhere out in the darkness a bell began to ring.

I was overcome with the sense that I must get up and step out the window, but my skin crawled at the thought of putting my feet down on the floor. In the suffocating darkness I could not be sure there was a floor.

Just as I could not bear the suspense any longer, something cold and clammy brushed against my face. That's when I screamed. I know, because I woke myself up.

My armpits were soaked and the waxy leaf of one of my wife's latest plant projects was stuck to my forehead. I must have slumped over into the plant stand when I fell asleep. It took a minute before I realized that the phone was ringing, sounding like an echo from the terror I had just left. Fortunately the lamp was still on, or I don't think I could have made myself get out of the chair to move toward the phone.

Groggily I lifted the receiver and mumbled, "Heywo."

"Is this the preacher? Speak up, I can't hear you," said a raspy voice. I could hear shouts and what sounded like glass breaking in the background.

"Yeah, this is Scott Daniels. Who's this?" A shiver shot down my spine as I wondered what kind of bad news arrived after midnight.

The voice sounded impatient and slightly slurred. "Preacher, we need you down here right now. He's going to shoot himself."

"Who's going to shoot himself? Who is this?"

"Come on, there's no time to waste. This is Billy Simpson. We're at the Legion hall. Now, are you coming or not?"

"Who's going to shoot . . . ?" The phone clicked in my ear. "Now what am I supposed to do?" I often talk to myself in moments of crisis.

"Who was that?"

I spun around, startled by the sleepy voice behind me. There stood my wife, Sandy, rubbing her eyes with both fists like a little girl.

"I'm not sure. I mean, it was Billy Simpson calling from the American Legion hall. You know, Connie's husband. I was sound asleep when the phone rang and when I answered it he started babbling about how somebody's going to shoot himself and to get right down there." I didn't quite grasp why I was the one being summoned. I'm a minister, not a sheriff.

"Are you going? Scott, it's the middle of the night." I know it's not nice to say, but Sandy could whine like one of the kids.

"I guess I'm going. What else can I do?"

"Well, it sounds like something for the police. Why don't you call them. It's their job, not yours. You wouldn't know what to do with a gun if it landed on your head." She had a point, but at the same time her words made me feel defensive.

"Maybe I will go down and see what they want with me. I can always call the police from there. Matter of fact, they're all probably too drunk to have thought of it." I shook my head, thinking of this strange new area I had landed in, with its picturesque scenery and peculiar people.

Sandy didn't sound too convinced. "Well, at least put on a jacket." Like that would stop a bullet.

"You're not my mother, Sandy. I know when to wear a jacket." I didn't intend to sound mean, but the whole situation had me nervous and upset. Anyway, I was sleeping in the family room because she and I were in a difficult period, as I liked to call it. It would do her good to sleep by herself for a while and see how she liked it.

She looked hurt. "You're right. I'm sorry. Of course you have to go, Scott." She took a step toward me.

I wasn't ready to give in quite yet, although I was acting meaner than I actually felt. So I stomped out to the garage without giving her a goodbye kiss, trying to act like a man with a mission. In reality, I was a very frightened man with no idea what I was going to do when I reached the American Legion hall down in the Potomac Valley town of Westwood where somebody or other had a gun and was threatening to use it.

As I backed the car out of the garage, I began to regret not having put on that jacket. The night was chilly and I could see tendrils of ground fog laying low across the road that wound its way into the valley below. We lived on the crest of Horse Rock Mountain, and although I could see the lights of town twinkling down beside the river, there were no streetlights from here to there.

I don't mind admitting that I'm afraid of the dark, especially after having the spooky window-with-mist dream again. It had been years since the last time, and I couldn't figure out why it was back.

As slowly as I drove, it still seemed almost no time before I stopped at the one traffic light in Westwood. The street was deserted except for a dirty yellow tomcat poking around near Jensen's Grocer and Lunch Counter. While waiting for the light like it was the middle of rush hour, I felt a pang of guilt over the way I had treated Sandy. It seemed like something was always making me snappy lately, but I couldn't put my finger on it. Without knowing why, I wanted to get in my digs at her over the smallest things. Maybe it was just all the changes of a new job, a new town, and a new baby.

When the light changed, I drove another block and took a sharp right turn at the Legion hall, the social center of the town, came into view. The parking lot in the rear was deserted except for two pickups and an old Cadillac. I parked my Datsun and went up to the plywood door marked *Bar Members Only*. All the way down I had been trying to guess what awaited me and why Billy thought I could do something about it. Knowing it was too late to back out now, I pushed open the door.

Inside I found a gloomy hallway. From the far end I could hear first shouting then murmuring voices. It reminded me of parents trying to stop their child's tantrum in the middle of church. I headed toward the sound.

As I stepped into the dim lighting, one of the voices became louder and more belligerent. It had a high-pitched tone that grated on my nerves and made my stomach churn.

"Stay away, all of you! Anybody tries to grab this and they'll get it right along with me."

I looked along the length of the battered bar toward the voice. My mouth dropped open. The voice belonged to an acne-covered kid with scraggly, dirty brown hair. He sat in a wheelchair parked between two pool tables in the back of the room.

He was the skinniest kid I had ever seen. He looked all the more scrawny in a sleeveless jungle camouflage shirt that revealed bony arms, one of which had a fierce tattoo of an eagle and underneath it the word *Mother* in blue letters. Gripped tightly with both hands, the huge pistol the boy waved made him look even smaller.

A big, beer-bellied man with a shiny bald head, wearing a stained white apron stretched taut across his wide middle, stood at the far end of the bar literally gnashing his teeth. Two other men, looking frightened and helpless, cowered in the corner beyond the man with the apron. Catty-cornered across the pool table I spied two more men. One looked to be about fifty and had close-cropped salt and pepper hair and toughened, weather-beaten skin. Next to him stood a man in his mid-thirties with thick black hair and a long, droopy mustache that made him look like an Old West desperado.

The older man had one hand stretched across the corner pocket toward the boy with the gun. The younger man was pulling at the other's shoulder as if to stop him from reaching any further. In that glance everyone seemed frozen in a bizarre painting.

For some reason I decided to see if anyone else lurked in the corner to my right. As I took a step forward, my foot hit against something hard. A beer mug skittered noisily across the floor until it hit the metal post of a bar stool and shattered. Everybody jumped, including me.

"What was that?" The gun swung toward me, until it pointed straight at my chest. "Who are you and what do you want?"

There was a bad taste in my throat as I tried to regain my balance. The kid's voice became even more shrill.

"Stay where you are. Don't move, or I'll use this thing!"

All I could see was the gun. I felt like vomiting.

"It's all right, Joey. It's the preacher. I asked him to come." The man with the big mustache spoke in a calm voice I recognized the raspy voice from the phone call that had set me on this fool's mission.

I tore my eyes away from the gun and saw the older man staring, his mouth set in a grim line. The one with the big mustache came over to me, his bloodshot eyes looking sad. As he stuck out his hand, the smell of beer engulfed me.

"I'm Billy Simpson. Thanks for coming, Preacher."

"What's going on here?" My voice was quivering.

"I didn't know who else to call, so I figured since Joey here is a member of your church, you could talk some sense into him." Billy's voice was steadier and quieter than it had been over the phone.

I swallowed hard since the fear was still clawing at my throat. My legs were weak. That gun looked bigger and bigger.

"What's the matter with . Joey, you said his name was?"

"Yeah, Joey McCrady. You mean you never met him before?" Billy chewed on an end of his mustache for a moment. "That's his dad over there." He nodded his head in the direction of the man with the military haircut.

My head started to spin. This kid was pointing a gun at his own father. What was I supposed to do? I stalled for time by staring at the little red lines that criss-crossed Billy's cheeks under the black stubble of his whiskers. Some went up over the bridge of his nose, too. His whole face looked bloodshot.

"He's mad at me." I hadn't noticed the older man come over. Glancing at his son in the wheelchair, he then nervously wiped his palms on the front of his khaki work pants before offering one to me to shake.

I gave it a tentative squeeze. I couldn't think of anything to say except, "It's nice to meet you."

"I don't get to church much, Preacher. My wife and I thought you might have come out to the house by now to see Joey, what with him and his condition." He gave a resigned shrug of the shoulders. His voice sounded tired, very tired.

"No, I'm sorry, I've never made it out there." I knew that *out there* was way back in the hollows of Hampshire County. One of the ministers from the next town, an old-timer, had told me that those hills were filled with families that were like the clans of yesteryear. There were brothers and cousins and uncles scattered throughout the small towns and villages that crept up the sides of the mountains and foothills. I had no idea as to how to make myself feel at home with them, so I stayed away.

"I think it's all the beer talking," Billy said.

"Yeah, he gets like this sometimes." Mr. McCrady shook his head as he continued. "I bring him down here most nights in my truck about seven or so. Then I come back later and take him home. He drinks a little bit, shoots pool all night, and makes like a tough guy."

He ran his hands through the stubble on top of his head. "Tonight he's all mad because I can't get the money to buy him a motorized wheelchair. Says he's tired of pushing himself around, that we don't love him at all, that he's no good to anybody since his accident. I tell you, Preacher, he's got a temper, but I ain't seen him get this bad before."

While my dizzy mind chewed this over, I snuck a peak at Joey. He looked for all the world like a little boy playing cowboys, aiming the gun around the room and pretending to shoot the bad guys. Unfortunately, there was no mistaking the gun for a toy, and I was in a position to be one of the bad guys.

"Where did he get the gun?" I asked. I really wanted to know what on earth his father was thinking bringing his son down to a bar every night, especially when he looked to be only seventeen, and in a wheelchair at that. But I got the distinct impression that I would be the only one in the room asking that question.

"Oh, it's his gun," offered Billy. Mr. McCrady nodded as Billy went on. "He brings it with him sometimes. Shows it off, talks big, thinks he's impressing girls, that kind of stuff. But tonight he decides to get fired up at his dad and says he's going to shoot himself because nobody cares."

"Hey, shut up over there." Joey was panting, and I could see the sweat running into his eyes. It didn't make me feel any safer, especially when I noticed his arms starting to shake. "Who is that?"

"We already told you," shouted Mr. McCrady. "It's the preacher."

"I called him," said Billy. His voice remained steady. "I thought maybe you'd talk to him, Joey. Maybe he could tell you that what you're doing is stupid. You're going to hurt yourself and your momma, too, even more."

"This is no place for a preacher," shrieked Joey.

Amen to that, I thought to myself. The gun wavered at my face.

"Get out of here. Go on, you don't have a prayer with me, Preacher." Joey paused and started to giggle. "Did you hear that? You don't have a prayer. Hee, hee, a preacher without a prayer." He put the gun down on his lap and laughed like a second-grader at his own joke.

I could feel my face getting hotter, sure that it was bright red.

"Go on," Billy said quietly behind me. "Go on over and talk to him."

I couldn't feel my feet anymore, and my arms were tingling. *This can't be happening to me*, I thought. Two nightmares in one night isn't fair.

I got one foot to move toward the pool table finally. "Joey?" The tentative squeak sure didn't sound like my voice.

Joey's giggling had stopped and the gun was back in his fists as he tracked my unsteady walk to the pool table.

"I don't need no preacher. How many times do I got to say it?" His eyes were wide as he gave a careless wave with the gun. "Go on, get out of here."

Two more steps and I leaned hard against the pool table. I felt a hand on my shoulder.

"Take it easy." It was Billy, and his words made me feel even more nervous. It must have been obvious that I had no idea of what to do and no stomach for the task. I had to get a grip on myself.

Now that I was closer I could see the urine bag strapped to the side of the wheelchair. The fatigue pants couldn't hide the fact that Joey's legs were no bigger around than my arms.

"I said, what are you staring at?" Joey blustered, looking embarrassed. I had been gawking so hard I must have missed the question the first time.

"I'm sorry, I didn't mean to stare. I guess I'm not sure what to say," I offered.

Joey misunderstood. "I don't need your pity, Preacher. Now I'm not going to tell you again, get out of here."

To my horror I realized that the gun was pointing directly at my forehead. My head started to spin as that monstrous hole at the end of the barrel absorbed all the oxygen in the room. My breath was coming in frightened gasps, and my feet acted like they had a will of their own. Before my left foot touched the floor, I heard loud yells.

"Don't!"

"Stop!"

"Look out!"

The shouts came from all directions. Suddenly, my whole body went numb. I heard a high-pitched scream.

"You asked for it!"

Footsteps ran behind me. I pivoted to see what was going on, but it was too much. The big bald guy was running in slow motion, his mouth moving but no sound coming out. Everything rushed at me through a tunnel. The taste in my throat choked me, the room started to spin, and I felt myself falling.

I heard a last terrified scream, "Joey, no!" followed by the thunderous boom of the gun going off. My head smacked against the floor and the lights went out.

TWO

The lights hurt my eyes even though I squeezed them tightly closed. My head throbbed. Gradually I became aware of a shrill keening that went on endlessly. It made me wonder if Joey would ever run out of breath. It stopped abruptly when I felt a hand gently shaking my shoulder, bringing me back to consciousness.

"Preacher? You okay?"

I tried opening my eyes just a slit, but a bright light hurt them. Moving my head turned out to be a mistake also, as the nauseating effect of hitting the floor in a dead fall readily became all too apparent.

"Preacher, wake up. It's over." The voice was filled with concern.

"I can't see. What's that light?" I muttered.

"Sam," the voice bellowed right in my ear, sending more pain through every nerve ending, "kill your lights. Preacher can't see."

The lights went out and I managed to get my eyes open. I realized with a start that I was sitting in the cab of a pickup. Through the windshield I could see the back of the American Legion building. Another truck with its motor running was pointed toward where I sat. I turned my head slightly and looked into Billy's sad brown eyes. I blinked a few times before I could ask, "What happened? Where am I?"

"You're in my truck, Preacher. You fainted. Are you going to be all right?"

I didn't believe it. I had fainted. I've never fainted in my life. I must have been staring because Billy asked again, "Are you sure you're all right?" He sounded weary.

"Yeah. I'm more embarrassed than anything. My head hurts, but everything seems to work."

Billy turned and walked to the other truck. After he had

a few words with the driver, it pulled away. Billy stayed, standing in the gloom for a moment. The clock on the dashboard said 3:15. *Good grief, how long had I been out?*

Gingerly I felt the knot on my head, while Billy came back to the open window. "You going to make it?" he asked with a slight smile.

"Yeah, I guess I wasn't much help in there. I feel pretty stupid about the whole thing. I don't even know what happened."

"Joey shot himself." The smile had vanished.

"What?"

"Shot himself right in the leg. It's not more than a flesh wound. Of course, he never felt it because he's paralyzed from the waist down. But it figures."

I wasn't following too well. "What figures?"

Billy tugged on one end of his droopy mustache. "He wanted to show his old man. That kid gets his parents to do anything he wants." Shaking his head he continued, "This has got to be the stupidest trick he ever pulled, though."

I leaned back in the seat, trying to absorb what I was hearing. "How is he?" Then it dawned on me to ask, "And how did I get out here?"

"The rescue squad came and rushed him out of there with sirens and lights and the whole bit. But I think he's going to be fine. There wasn't even much blood, and none of the boys in the squad will squeal on where he was."

"Squeal?" I sputtered. "An underage kid is in a bar in the middle of the night and ends up shooting himself, and you're worried that nobody is going to squeal?" *What planet did these people come from?*

Billy's eyes flashed. "You got a lot to learn, Preacher. I called you because I thought you might understand."

"Understand? C'mon, Billy, what I understand about all this is that I don't have a clue about any of it."

Billy's smile caught me off guard. "Well, at least you're honest, Preacher. That's a good start. It was me. I dragged you out here before the police came so you wouldn't end up in any official report."

"Thanks, I think." I rubbed my eyes, which by now felt like they must be as bloodshot as Billy's. I let out a big sigh.

"Don't be so hard on yourself," said Billy. "Who knows what would have happened? You were the only sober one there. You tried." He patted me on the shoulder and opened the truck door.

My whole body felt stiff as I climbed down. "By the way," I asked, "how did Joey end up in a wheelchair?"

Billy shook his head as he began relating the story. "He had an accident about eighteen months ago. He liked to ride his dirt bike out in the woods. He'd go by himself, which is dumb enough, but he would also go places out there that his parents told him were too dangerous. Just had to show them he didn't have to listen, I guess. Well, one evening he didn't come home. His mom called out the McCrady clan, and they went looking for him. Found him near Turner's Run, lying there unconscious beside his bike. He doesn't even remember what happened, but knowing him, he probably tried some fool stunt. Now look at him, he has to pay for it for the rest of his life."

Billy ran his fingers through his long hair. "You know, Preacher, a lot of people around here figured it was a shame and all, but they said the boy got what he deserved. A hell-raiser now stuck in his own hell. Personally, I have trouble believing that if there is a God he'd be like that. I mean, doing that to a young kid even if he did deserve it."

I listened intently, thinking again of how far I had to go before I would understand the people of this area. Each one had a story of family, fate, and folly all woven together that would take me forever to figure out. I realized that Billy was staring at me as though he expected a response.

"I don't think God did it to Joey. I think Joey did it to Joey." I rubbed my sore head and winced. "I think the floor sure did it to me."

Billy laughed. "I admire you for coming, Preacher. That

was a nasty situation. Even if you didn't know what to do, you didn't back down.

"I'll tell you what," he continued. "One of these days when your head is feeling better, would you like to go hunting or fishing with me?"

Here it came. I never thought of myself as much of a man's man. I wasn't very good at sports, although I loved them, and I was never a fisherman or a hunter. I was always afraid of how that made me look to other men.

"To tell you the truth, Billy, I've never done either one. I feel silly, being here in the middle of all these mountains and streams and forests and not fishing or hunting." There, I said it.

"Yeah, well, Connie's always told me I'd rather fish or hunt than be with her." Billy abruptly stopped talking and walked around to the back of the truck.

I didn't know whether to follow or not. I wanted to hear more, but I didn't want to step on his pride, or whatever had made him shut up. I decided to press on and walked around to the tailgate.

Billy looked up as I approached and said with a half-hearted laugh, "I could sure go for a beer now. Connie said that's the other thing I'd rather be doing, making love to a beer mug."

I stood there waiting. I had met Billy only briefly once before when I first came to Westwood. His wife, Connie, sang in the choir, helped with Sunday school, and had apparently dragged Billy along to the reception for the new minister following my first service.

As he came through the line, Billy gave me a firm hand-shake, looked me in the eye, and said, "You have a good way with words, Preacher." It was the only time I ever saw him in church.

Billy kicked at the gravel beside the truck tire and, keeping his head down, said softly, "Connie kicked me out."

It caught me by surprise. Connie brought their three-year-old son with her to church each week and always smiled whenever I asked her how she was doing. I never thought to look beyond the smile to see if things were really okay. I felt vaguely uneasy, wondering if I should have known before now that one of my parishioners was in this much trouble. In a church this small in a town this small, everybody else probably already knew.

"Why did she do that?" I finally asked.

Billy studied me for a long moment, as if to size me up. Then he shrugged. "Well, it's always been kind of a funny relationship," he said.

I wasn't sure I was up to marriage counseling after all that had occurred in the last few hours, but Billy seemed ready to talk.

"I don't think I really wanted to get married. I enrolled in Eastern Panhandle State, but in the first semester Connie got pregnant. I felt like I had to make an honest woman out of her, and I didn't want to keep driving back and forth every weekend to see her." He looked at me as though that were explanation enough.

"I don't get it. You said it's a funny relationship. Lots of people have gotten married like that."

Billy looked at me sideways, head still down, as he continued to scuff at the loose stones.

"I don't know why I'm telling you any of this. I'm not much for preachers and churches. They're for old ladies that can't handle the real world," he challenged.

"You might be right, Billy. Churches aren't always my favorite places to be." *And how,* I muttered under my breath.

He gave me a funny look, opened his mouth, and then closed it. We were silent for a moment, then he continued his story. "Connie's always been on me about wasting my life. She says I'm too smart to just goof off all the time and play in the woods with my guns or my fishing rod. She wants more kids, but that first one was enough for me. Why make the same mistake twice, I always say. Then she gets upset about me calling Mikey a mistake. She screams at me and says that I never loved her, that all I love is hunting and fishing. Or drinking."

I stayed silent, waiting.

"It's this place, Preacher. It gets to me. I was born and raised here in these mountains and valleys. I know them like I know my own body. A man can go off in these hills and be by himself, forget about the rest of the world. But I'm not stupid, Preacher. I know it can be a prison, too. People expect you to be this or that, and that's all they'll let you be. The horizons are small, and I've got itchy feet. But I don't have the guts to change anything. I want to stay, but I want to leave. Sometimes I blame Connie and Mikey for tying me down here. Then I hate myself, which makes me want to get out all the more."

"What were you going to study?" I knew Billy worked for the town street department and helped on the garbage truck, but I never guessed there had been college in his past.

"Art."

I hoped the darkness hid my surprise. I also felt a sense of awe at being allowed into such a private, personal world. I knew as a minister that it was part of the job, but it still amazed me that someone like Billy would let me into his secret domain. I was beginning to wonder why I had been so quick to pigeonhole him myself.

Billy leaned against the truck and looked up at the stars. "This isn't making a lot of sense, I know."

"What kind of art?" My curiosity was peaked.

Billie ignored my question. "You know, I don't know where I'd go if I did get out of here. I'll tell you this, I love my boy. That hurts the most. I know Connie will let me see him whenever I want, but he's my son. I could have shown him the way out of here. Now I'll be lucky just to see him." He slammed a fist against the side of the pickup.

"Connie thinks she's going to find something better. Well, I know she deserves it. She said she was tired of beer breath and my coming in late or not at all. She said she didn't want Mikey to have to grow up with a no-good daddy." Billy's eyes blinked rapidly. He hastily wiped at them with one hand.

I thought about pointing out to him what he had said earlier about not being sure he wanted to be married in the first place, but I thought better of it.

"Preacher, there's things in me that just ache to come out, like I might burst if they don't. I was first in my high school class, did you know that? Now I dig ditches, sweep streets, and pick up garbage. It gives me drinking money and helps pay some bills at home along with Connie's paycheck. And it lets me do what I want with my hobbies. That's another thing Connie is all mad about. All that money for paints and photography equipment."

My puzzlement must have showed, because Billy quickly opened the toolbox mounted behind the truck cab, carefully lifted out two rectangular objects, walked around, and held them out to me. They were lightweight. I turned them over and realized they were paintings, very good paintings. I held them up to catch more of the glow from the streetlights and saw a stylized *B.S.* in the bottom right-hand corner of each one.

Giving a low whistle, I asked, "You did these?"

"Yeah," was all Billy said.

I looked at them more closely. The first painting was of a high mountain valley, a scene of quiet beauty and solitude, but painted with powerful, sure strokes. In the center of the meadow stood a doe, alert and looking out from the picture with hauntingly gentle eyes. The other painting was of mountain flowers done in soft pastels.

"These are beautiful, Billy. Very good. You should do more with your talent."

Billy ripped the two paintings out of my hands and threw them across the parking lot.

"I'll give you *should!*" he yelled at the tumbling canvases. "Stay out of my business, Preacher," he scornfully flung over his shoulder as he ran around the cab, jumped in, slammed the door, and started the engine with a roar. With tires spitting gravel, he made a wide turn so that the oversized tires ran over the paintings, and sped out of the lot, leaving me standing, stunned, in a cloud of dust.

I took one step after the retreating taillights, then turned and walked slowly back to the paintings while trying to make sense out of all that Billy had told me. The floral arrangement painting was a mess, with big, black tire marks obliterating most of the flowers, leaving only one corner untouched. The other had fared better, miraculously, with just a small tear in the canvas between the eyes of the deer. Bewildered, I picked them both up, walked shakily to the car, climbed in, and started back up the mountain for home.

As I drove along the winding road, a picture of my wife, Sandy, came to my mind. Billy's words had stirred something inside of me: a picture of the two of us, Sandy's long red hair flowing over her shoulders and me looking into her green eyes as they smiled back into mine. We half lay, half sat on the couch in the living room of her parents' house after coming home from a date. The buttons of her blouse were undone and I could feel my whole body shaking with excitement. We had dated for two months, and each night the kisses grew longer and the touching more desperate. Now I was about to enter the promised land. Except that all of a sudden my mind filled with dread. I felt like I couldn't breathe and abruptly I sat up. Sandy looked at me with a puzzled expression. I groped for words to explain what was wrong.

After a long pause I finally said, "I think we should do this when we're married."

Sandy's eyes grew wide. "Scott, is that a proposal?"

Gulp. *I sure hope not.* "No, I just meant I don't want to hurt you or make you hate me, or something."

She looked confused by my feeble explanation.

A movement up ahead along the side of the road drew my attention back to my driving. *Must be a deer,* I thought. *Better slow down.* The ground fog still hugged the road, giving me that familiar creepy feeling down my spine.

As I drew even with the spot where I thought I saw

movement, there was a rustling in the bushes close to the road. Suddenly a figure burst out of the undergrowth and dashed into the path of my car. It was a man, and as he reached the middle of the road he turned and looked into the glare of my headlights like a trapped animal.

I slammed on the brakes. One side of his face was normal, with one frightened eye fixed on me. The other side was drawn, the corner of his mouth pulled toward his ear, the eyelid drooping over a dull yellowish eyeball, the skin on his cheek sagging and wrinkled. It was Zeke. How had he escaped?

THREE

"You kids get out of there. Worship is about to start."
Oh no, somebody caught us.
"Scott, we better go."
"I don't want to go, Sandy. I like it here."

I had my face pressed into her thick, auburn hair that smelled like strawberries. It swept across one eye and down to her shoulders. We had been making out in the darkened kitchenette next to the Christian Ladies of the Church lounge, which was well known to be off limits to sixteen-year-old boys trying to create passionate moments with their fifteen-year-old girlfriends.

Sandy giggled and pushed me away. Her slender body had curves in all the right places, and I especially liked the miniskirt that showed off her long legs. I didn't know which was better, seeing her in that or in the tight bell-bottom jeans that first drew my attention during the rehearsals for last Christmas Eve's choral program.

"Quit staring, Romeo. We're supposed to go out there and sing a duet before the communion service today, remember?"

"Well, how about if we sneak out after we sing and find somewhere to pick up where we left off?"

"Scott, we can't do that."

"Come on, yes we can. There's going to be some boring sermon, and then everybody will sit there looking all serious and sad while they pretend to feel sorry for Jesus as they eat milk and cookies."

Sandy stared at me openmouthed. "You shouldn't make fun like that. And it's your own dad up there preaching. You shouldn't talk about him like that, either."

She patted me on my steel-belted radial love handles

bulging over the waist of my good pants. "Feels like you already got your share of milk and cookies, little boy."

I rolled my eyes at her. "Not the kind I'd like to have, little girl."

I marveled at how comfortable I felt with her while, at the same time, feeling a pang of guilt. She was right, I was being hard on my dad and hard on the church, but I just didn't seem to fit in with either one. Everyone expected me to follow in my father's footsteps, but from where I stood, his footsteps led nowhere.

"Get moving, you two, the service is about to begin."

The worrywart of a choir director, Edith Montrose, waggled her finger to shoo us down the long hallway leading to the new addition to the church building. It contained the recently completed sanctuary my dad had knocked himself out for so long and so hard to get built.

The congregation was already singing the first hymn when Sandy and I found our seats near the front of the choir loft which sat off to one side in the cavernous, brightly lit room. At the front stood the big wooden communion table laden with the elements for the sacrament, covered with a white cloth and looking like a big coffin with a ghostly shroud.

Sandy leaned over to whisper in my ear, "Your dad looks tired, Scott. Is he feeling okay?"

I shrugged my shoulders in response. I knew that getting this building project completed had taken a lot out of him. I resented all the time he spent with church business, and I really got steamed when my mother didn't have the guts to tell him to slow down. He missed my Spring Festival band concert where I had my big solo on the sax because the head of the building committee called and said there was a fight with the architect or some such nonsense. If he didn't care, why should I?

The singing stopped and I half listened as my father began to speak. He was telling a story to make his point. I always liked hearing him tell stories, and I reluctantly admitted that he was good at it. In fact, part of me still wished for those days when I was a little boy huddled under the covers, listening while he spun out a tale from the Bible or, for a special treat, one of his own made-up stories. I missed those days when life was so much simpler.

Looking around, I didn't see too many other sixteen-year-olds in the gray-haired crowd. At the age of fourteen a half dozen of us had joined the church. My dad's age, fifty-two, didn't help keep most of us around, or maybe the rest of the church didn't know what to do with us either. At any rate, my peers went through the ritual, then disappeared. Sandy was one of the few young people who seemed to enjoy being here. I did not have a choice in the matter. My parents said I would go to church, period. No wonder my sister chose to go to college a thousand miles away. I couldn't wait until it was my turn. *Let's get this duet over with*, I thought, returning to the matter at hand. *Then get me out of here.*

From the choir loft I could see my mother in her usual seat, all alone in a long pew near the front, eyes fixed adoringly on my dad. She wore a dull-colored dress that must have been in style when I was a baby. Her gray hair strayed out of the braid that she wound around the top of her head every morning and carefully unwound and brushed one hundred strokes every evening while sitting on the side of their bed listening to my dad read to her from the Psalms.

I squeezed Sandy's hand and decided my time would be better spent studying her. I could tell she was totally absorbed in the story by the way she sucked on her upper lip, eyes narrowed, like she was hearing all this for the first time. She half turned and gave me a smile although I could tell she still listened to the sermon. It had taken me six agonizing weeks to work up the courage to ask her out. As she turned back to give her full attention to my father, I whispered a thank-you toward the ceiling.

Suddenly the congregation let out a collective gasp. In the same instant Sandy covered her mouth with one hand and leaned forward. I followed her terrified look up to the pulpit and instantly felt my heart in my mouth. My dad lay sprawled across the open Bible, his notes fluttering toward the floor, while one arm feebly waved at them like he was trying to catch them before they landed. His face was pasty white and only a gurgling sound came out of his mouth as it continued to open and close as though he were still speaking. For a moment the rest of us sat there deathly quiet.

Then chaos erupted. Someone screamed, "Get a doctor!" while the ushers urgently dashed up the center aisle. Mr. Brown, the organist, crashed both hands down on the keys, making the organ howl in protest. I let go of Sandy's hand and started to push my way through an aisle rapidly clogging with people trying to see what was going on up front or heading for the exits.

In all the confusion I could barely see the braid on the top of my mother's head as she made her way toward my father, now gently stretched out on the floor by the ushers. As I fought to get through to them, I could hear above the din the wail of a siren approaching the church. *Thank God somebody called an ambulance*, I thought.

When I got to the front, I could see my mother kneeling at my father's side, softly stroking his forehead. One look at his drawn, pale face made my stomach lurch. I wanted to step closer to kneel beside him too, but instead I remained rooted to the spot by some giant invisible hand. Did I have any right to be with him, I wondered, after being so peevish and callous toward his love for the church?

I was nudged out of the way by one of the medics pulling a stretcher. I backed up until the little alcove leading into the choir room hid me from view. My father never moved or spoke as the medics worked on him, and my mother never let go of his hand. I wanted to run over to them and take hold of his other hand, but I was afraid that if I did he would see right through me and know I wasn't good enough for him. Or worse, that I would find out it was too late to say anything.

As they wheeled him away, I noticed the ushers herding the rest of the people out of the building, telling them to go home as there was nothing more to do except pray. Trembling in the darkened corner, I wanted desperately to pray, too, but no words came.

"Please God," I whispered. But that's as far as I could get.

When everything was quiet, I cautiously stepped out of the shadows. Seeing my father's notes scattered on the floor under the communion table, I got down on my knees and crawled around the now deserted sanctuary picking them up. Cradling them in both hands, I carried the papers up to the pulpit and carefully laid them there on the big Bible where he could find them when he returned. It was all I could think to do for him.

I decided to drive the family station wagon home, but halfway there I changed my mind and headed for the hospital. When I walked into the intensive care unit waiting room, to my surprise I saw Sandy and Edith Montrose sitting there with my mother.

Sandy came to meet me and give me a big hug. Then she said, "I was worried. Nobody knew what happened to you. You just disappeared."

I started to tell her about hiding in the alcove, then stopped. What if she didn't understand? Or worse, what if she scolded me for not having the guts to be there? I wasn't ready to trust her that much.

"I, uh, I thought he might need some stuff from home." I could feel my face burning as I realized there was nothing in my hands to back up my excuse.

Sandy kissed me on the cheek. "It's okay, Scott. I understand. Come talk to your mother."

She led me over to where Edith Montrose talked quietly with my mother. Mom looked ten years older all of a sudden. The worry in her eyes made me want to cry, but instead I sat down across from her and stared while waiting for her to look my way.

"Did anyone call your sister?" asked Sandy.

When Mom didn't answer I muttered, "I don't know."

Except for Sandy being there, I felt sorry I had come. Obviously it didn't matter to my mother if I was there or not.

Mrs. Montrose leaned over to pat me on the knee. "The doctors said to call any family, Scott. Don't worry, though, everything is in God's hands."

I resisted the urge to smack her hand away. I could feel my legs starting to shake as the fear grabbed me again. God's hands hadn't stopped this from happening, had they? And my hands certainly weren't much help.

"Mom?" My voice sounded like I was being strangled.

She shook her head without a word, while her red, chapped hands kept twisting the corner of a tattered handkerchief around and around. For a moment I hated myself for being ashamed of her outdated dress mended in a half dozen places and the second-hand coat with the frayed sleeves she wore. Maybe she didn't have any choice in the matter.

After a while Sandy came over, sat on the arm of my chair, and held my hand.

"Scott, I'm sorry, but I've got to go. Somebody called in sick today at our store and I need to go help my dad." She leaned over and kissed me on the cheek. "I'll call later. I'll be praying for your dad."

I hated to let her go. As she left, a short man with hound dog eyes dressed in a white coat came in and impatiently excused himself. "Are you the Daniels family? The nurse said you were waiting. I'm Doctor Hendricks."

The guy's attitude made my skin crawl. He led my mother and me into a tiny room with three chairs and no windows and quickly closed the door. Before we were seated he began.

"Mrs. Daniels, let me tell it to you straight. Your husband is in bad shape. Right now we're keeping him alive with machines."

"No . . . no . . . no. . . ." Mom shook her head, tears streaming down both cheeks.

The doctor looked uncomfortable, shifting from one foot to the other. I felt like an actor standing outside the scene, helplessly watching some jerk of a stranger destroy my mother's world. I awkwardly patted her on the shoulder as it dawned on me that my world was coming apart too, ready or not.

"I need to talk to my daughter, Doctor." Mom seemed to rally a little. "She can help me decide about Daddy."

I felt a pang of jealousy. Why wasn't I good enough to talk to about . . . Dad. *Why did she still insist on calling him Daddy,* I wondered.

"Mrs. Daniels, I'm afraid there isn't much time." His tone actually seemed to have softened a little. "Your husband is suffering a great deal. The stroke was triggered by a tumor in his brain. He must have been feeling it long before now. Didn't he say anything?"

Mom looked bewildered. "No, just the usual headaches from all the strain of his work."

"Well, I don't know how he could have kept it from you. I've seen cases like this before . . ." He cut himself off abruptly as he stared hard at the top of my mother's bowed head.

"Oh, Daddy," she sobbed. "I can't lose you. I just can't. You're all I have." Her face crumbled a little more with each passing moment.

Panic rose in my chest. I wanted to get out of this place, and I desperately looked around for the door as the doctor spoke again.

"Mrs. Daniels, somebody has to decide. The longer he lives, the worse the pain becomes. We can give him drugs, but eventually even they won't help."

Every word cut into me like a dagger. Just an hour before, I had been wanting to get away from him and what he stood for in that ugly church. Now . . . now I couldn't think beyond this horrible little room and this doctor's brutal words.

"Would you like to see him?"

The question startled me. I hadn't even thought about it, to be honest. Mom seemed to have gone numb. Her eyes filled with pain, but no tears flowed as she nodded her head.

"Mom, I can't. I don't . . . I just can't."

She didn't say a word, but stood up and slowly walked out of the room. I followed in time to see her and Edith Montrose go through the big doors into the intensive care unit. I tried not to think about what they were seeing while I stared out the window. What kind of son would refuse to see his own father's suffering and dying? *I'm nothing but a coward,* I told myself over and over. *Nothing but a coward.*

I didn't turn around when I heard them come back from their visit. Footsteps approached where I stood with my back to the door.

"Scott?" Mrs. Montrose spoke. I turned around. "Your mother wants to see you out in the hall."

"Why?"

"She just asked me to tell you to come out, please." She turned on her heel and walked out.

As I came through the door my mother grabbed me tightly around both wrists. She had a frightened look in her eyes, and her hair flew wildly in all directions from her braid as though she had been pulling on it.

"Scott, I can't do it." Her desperate voice stung me. She held on as she continued. "You have to do it. You're the man now. I can't, I just can't do it."

I tried to pull away, but her grip only grew tighter. Her body rocked back and forth while she held me with her eyes.

"Mom, please," I pleaded. "Don't do this. Please don't do this to me." I felt like I couldn't breathe.

"You have to do it. Tell the doctor what to do. I can't. Daddy didn't even know me. He's in terrible pain, but I can't do it." She ended in a wrenching sob that echoed in the hallway. "Don't make him suffer. Please make it stop. Please make it stop."

She leaned against me, and I could feel her tears soaking through my shirt. I freed one hand and put it on her braid. Suddenly she jerked away from my hand and grabbed the other one in both of hers.

Her voice came out in a fierce whisper. "Promise me, Scott. Promise your mother. You tell Daddy you love him. Do you hear me? You tell Daddy that you love him before you kill him."

I don't think she realized what she said, either then or later. But I have never been able to erase those words from my mind.

I went into the intensive care unit in a fog. How could I go in, how could I not go in? My father writhed under the relentless glare of white lights. His eyes looked glassy as he moaned unintelligibly. I leaned over him and tried to say it. I tried, but I couldn't. All I could say to the hovering nurse was, "Please. Please, put him out of his pain. Let Daddy go." That's all.

FOUR

The present time
"Zeke?"

He stared with one good eye into the headlights, then started to back away. I opened the car door and called to him again.

"Zeke, it's me, Scott Daniels. It's okay, I'm not going to hurt you." I held out my hands so that he could see them, and then I took a step toward him.

"How do I know you're not one of them?" Only one side of Zeke's face still functioned, so it looked like he talked out the side of his mouth. His hoarse voice carried a tone of distrust and despair.

"Zeke, don't you remember me? I came to visit the day you went into the home."

"My memory ain't so good since this blamed stroke." He self-consciously rubbed the sagging flesh on the left side of his face. "Who'd you say you were?"

"I'm the minister. I came with your daughter-in-law, Connie, and your grandson, Mikey."

At the mention of Mikey, his good side brightened noticeably. "Mikey's a good boy," he said. He studied my face as I came around the front of the car. "You're the preacher. You're supposed to help me."

"That's right. I want to help you, Zeke." It was like talking to a frightened child or a wounded animal. "What are you doing out here all alone?"

"Just taking a little midnight stroll, Preacher." One side of his mouth turned up in a grotesque smile.

I couldn't keep myself from laughing and decided to play along. "Well, it's a fine night for a walk. I was thinking of taking one myself."

I walked over, noticing that he shivered in the chilly air. He backed away a couple of steps.

"It's okay, Zeke, honest. I'm not going to hurt you." *This craggy, half man, half aberration is more skittish than a horse's shadow,* I thought.

"It's an insane asylum, you know that, don't you?" Zeke was half out of the glare of the headlights now, and the shadows gave his face a ghastly appearance, a lost creature from the underworld.

"Now, Zeke, you know better than that. C'mon, Mrs. Orr is supposed to go into Sunnyside next week. You remember her, don't you, from the church? Her son said it's just the right place for her, nice and friendly."

"Shows what you know," snorted Zeke, continuing to back away from me until his foot caught on a rock and he sprawled on the pavement. "Now look what you made me do, Preacher."

I ran the few steps to kneel beside him. "Are you okay, Zeke? That was a nasty fall. Here, let me help you."

"Don't talk to me like I'm a baby, Preacher. I was diggin' coal out of these hills when your mommy and daddy were still playing tonsil hockey in the back seat of a '49 Buick."

He pushed my hand away and attempted to stand. "That boy of Andrea Orr's is a complete waste of perfectly good dirt and oxygen. His mother's dying and all he wants to do is get rid of her, let somebody else take care of her because he can't be bothered."

What was the old fool ranting about now? All I wanted was to go home to my pouting wife and try to salvage something of this lost night.

"C'mon, Zeke, let me take you back home."

Zeke shakily drew himself up to his full height, the healthy side of his face a mask of bitterness.

"That place is not, and never will be, home, Preacher Boy. And I am not going back there, so just get back in your car and leave me be."

I put my hands on my hips and sighed. "No, I won't leave

you out here. You'll freeze before morning. How about if I take you on up to Billy and Connie's house? They can figure out what to do with you in the morning. Okay? Will you come with me there?"

Zeke slowly nodded his head and followed me back to the car. Not until I turned into their driveway did I remember Billy's news earlier in the evening. Maybe this wasn't such a good idea. Too late now. What else would I do with Zeke? Take him home with me?

The lights burned in the kitchen at the rear of the house. I'll admit I've always liked being around Connie, but when she came to the back door wearing only an oversized man's workshirt, her personality was not what captured my attention. The top two buttons were undone and I was rapidly and willingly losing the battle to keep my attention on her face. Her brown hair hung limply above her shoulders, outlining a face that bore the scars of adolescent acne and slightly protruding front teeth.

She opened the door, looking weary and worried. "Reverend? Is that you? Is something wrong? It's not Billy, is it?"

"No, no. I'm sorry to bother you, Connie." I turned around, expecting to see Zeke following close behind. Instead, he still sat in the car, staring glumly straight ahead. "It's Zeke. I found him out on the road and he refuses to go back to the home."

Connie shook her head. "That doesn't surprise me." Her face relaxed a little. "Excuse the way I'm dressed, Reverend. I wasn't expecting company at this hour."

"Hey, it's Scott, remember? Call me Scott, please."

She smiled. "I forgot. Scott, what are you doing out at this hour?"

"It's a long story."

"Well, let me talk to Zeke and get him into the house. I've got coffee on, so come in and sit for a while if you have the time."

She walked past me leaving the faint scent of Emeraude perfume and cigarettes stirring the air around me. Leaning into the open car window, she spoke in low tones to Zeke, who appeared to soften. I knew I shouldn't be looking as her shirt rode up in the back, but I looked anyway. That cup of coffee sounded better and better.

Later, as the three of us sat around the kitchen table, I told them about the earlier events at the American Legion. I couldn't help voicing my consternation at the McCrady family's lack of propriety and plain old common sense.

Up until that point Zeke listened in silence, sipping on his black coffee laced with whiskey which Connie reluctantly dug out of a corner cupboard. He sat his cup down with a loud thump on the formica.

"It's important to all of them that Joey be a man." He stood up. "I know where my bed is, Connie. I won't wake Mikey." With that he left the room without so much as a thank-you or an apology for his part in the evening's disruptions.

"Don't let him rattle you, Scott," said Connie. She now had on a bathrobe and reached into its pocket for a cigarette while letting out a big sigh. "I hope you don't mind, but since Billy left I'm back on these awful things."

It was nearly dawn, but I wanted to stay, to keep talking. I felt comfortable with Connie. Maybe I was too tired, but I also felt excited. We had been around each other frequently at church functions, and we related easily, laughing and joking with each other. This time felt different. I wanted more of it.

"Maybe I should get going," I said, without making a move to get up.

"You can stay, Scott. Talk to me some more, I could use the company." She studied me with eyes that promised they could secure all of my secrets as well as hide her own private sufferings.

"You didn't seem all that surprised to see Zeke turn up on your doorstep." I settled deeper into my chair.

"He's like his son, has a mind of his own. I think he felt he was doing Billy and me a favor by getting out of our hair. He knew things were rough between us and thought it might help if he wasn't around. So that's why he went to the home, but I know it's got to be like a prison to him. But once he makes up his mind there's no stopping him." She blew smoke at the ceiling. "Oh well, Mikey will be glad to see him."

"What . . . uh, I don't know how to ask this without sounding like an idiot. But Zeke's face, what caused . . . that?"

"The same thing that causes everything in Zeke's life— drinking. If you don't know by now, Zeke is not the favorite son of this town. He's been accused of everything from shoplifting to molesting little girls. Not exactly a shining example for Billy to point to at the little league games when he was a kid, wouldn't you say?" Connie got up and refilled both our cups.

"Anyway, one night some years back he got drunk and fell off the train trestle out behind the mill. Landed on his head. It's a wonder it didn't kill him. Believe me, nobody in this town would have missed him, including Billy. The bleeding in his brain caused a stroke that paralyzed half of his face."

"He said something about a stroke, but not the rest of it. Why did Billy take him in if they are so estranged?"

"Oh, Zeke doesn't live here. He just sleeps here when he knows Billy won't be around. Billy knows it, but he keeps his mouth shut. He won't admit it, but Billy really does have a big heart. He just can't make peace with his father." Matter-of-factly she added, "Well, I guess it's not a problem for his dad to sleep here now."

As Connie brushed the hair out of her face, I saw a tear in the corner of one eye. Before I thought about it, I reached my hand across the corner of the table and touched her arm. "I'm sorry."

She smiled and covered my hand with hers. "You're too nice, you know that? Out at all hours on your white horse, rounding up the heartless and the hopeless."

When I didn't return the smile, she quickly drew her hand away. "I'm sorry, I didn't mean to make fun."

"No, it's not that." I reluctantly took my hand off of her

arm. "I don't feel much like the white knight these days. I don't know, maybe I wasn't cut out for this kind of work."

"What makes you say that?" Connie covered her mouth with her hand and giggled. "Listen to me, sounding like a big shot and acting like you would want to confide in a nobody mountain hick like me."

"I like talking to you, Connie. It's been a long time since I could sit and tell somebody what I'm thinking about." I looked her right in the eye. "I'm glad it's you." Little alarms went off deep within me, but I managed to ignore them.

Connie blushed. "I know it's none of my business, but what about Sandy?"

"What about her? I don't mean to sound heartless, but have you ever felt lonely while sitting right next to somebody?" I listened to my words, wondering where they were coming from. But there was no going back.

Connie had a faraway look in her eyes. "Yeah."

"It's not like I have any friends to speak of, either. Maybe it's me, I don't know."

"I like you, Scott. You're . . . well, different."

I laughed. "That's me all right. Different."

"I'm sorry, I'm not very good with words." Connie looked at the floor and nervously patted her pockets, looking for another cigarette.

I stared at her for a long moment, then stood up.

"I'd better go."

Connie stood up, also. "I hope I didn't say anything wrong."

"No. Like I said, I like talking to you—a lot. Can I come back for more coffee? Soon?"

The front of her robe fell open slightly and my eyes couldn't resist. "Any time, Scott. And thanks."

"For what?"

"For listening, and for treating me like you cared. I haven't had much of that." She stood on her tiptoes to give me a kiss on the cheek. The feel of her body pressing lightly against mine sent my blood racing. I almost reached out to hold her close.

I felt my face getting hot. "I'd . . . you're welcome."

"Mommy?"

Mikey stood in the doorway rubbing sleep from his eyes.

"Oh Sweetie, did we wake you?" Connie went over to the boy and picked him up.

"I'm hungry, Mommy."

"Oh my goodness, it's 6:30!" She came back and put her hand on my arm. "I didn't know it was so late, or early, Scott. You'd better get home. Thanks again for bringing Zeke."

The morning sun chased away the last of the fog as I pulled into my own driveway at the top of Horse Rock Road. It felt like a year since I had been awakened from the nightmare and began my journey down the mountain. Sandy sat in her bathrobe in the breakfast nook, head on the table. She sat up abruptly when I closed the door.

"Honey, is that you?" She came around the counter, a worried look on her face.

"Yeah, it's me, the lone ranger nightrider of Western Maryland."

"What happened? I've been worried sick waiting for you to call."

I gulped. It never dawned on me to report in. "I got kind of busy."

"Let me make you some coffee. You must be exhausted."

Oddly, the opposite was true. My time with Connie had revived me.

"No thanks, I'm coffeed out."

Sandy gave me a puzzled look. "Where did you get coffee at this hour?"

"It's kind of a long story, and I would really like to climb into bed for a while. Preferably with you, Hon." The juices were humming.

Sandy came over and gave me a kiss. "Phew, where were you? You smell like cigarettes."

"Well, like I said, it's a long story. But I ended up at

Connie Simpson's house because I found her father-in-law out on the road."

"What? I heard she kicked Billy out. What's her no good father-in-law doing at her house?"

"I couldn't think of anyplace else to take him. It was okay with her. She gave me a cup of coffee and we chatted for a little bit. It's been rough on her, I guess, so I thought she might need to talk."

Sandy stepped away from me. "In the middle of the night? You mean you've been down there talking to her and never bothered to call and let me know you were okay?" She crossed her arms in front of her and gave me a chilly stare.

"I'm sorry, really I am, Sandy. The whole night has been crazy, believe me. I'd really like to just snuggle with you for a while." I held out my arms hopefully.

"Is that all you think about, Scott?"

That was not a good sign, I knew. "No, but it's what I'm thinking about now." Might as well keep trying.

"Scott, the kids will be up soon. Besides, you stink."

The juices drained away with a thud.

"Oh, and before I forget, Esther Savacini called a little while ago. She heard the call for the rescue squad on her scanner. She wanted to know if you had gone in the ambulance with Joey McCrady."

"She called this early? The woman has a radar receiver instead of a brain."

Esther Savacini was a royal pain. She made everything her business, and she went to great lengths to let me know it. Even at six in the morning, apparently. I wondered what she was saying about my fainting in the American Legion hall.

"Scott, she said there were gunshots. Are you sure you're all right?"

"I'm fine. Don't you think I'd be the first to know if I weren't?"

"You don't have to be so touchy, Scott. I'm just telling you what she said. Maybe she's trying to be helpful."

"Oh great, Sandy, why don't you jump on my back like she did." My emotions bubbled close to the surface.

Sandy turned her back on me and started banging pots and pans to make a breakfast I didn't want.

I had to admit as I lathered up in the shower that I did stink. Under the covers I shut my eyes against the sunlight, wishing I knew what was going on with Sandy. I heard the kids clamoring for apple juice and her tired voice shushing them so Daddy could sleep.

The image of Connie leaning over to talk to Zeke in the car came to mind. Then the feel of her lips on my cheek, her warmth against me. I shook my head.

"C'mon, Scott," I said out loud. "Get over it."

After all, I wasn't out there looking to have an affair. I knew what I was doing.

Didn't I?

FIVE

I was on my way to apologize to a dead woman. A little more than a week had passed since my encounters with Joey and Zeke. Now, as I drove the two-lane highway north to Cumberland's Divine Providence Convalescent Center, I dreaded seeing Andrea Orr. Her son had placed her there, rather than the Sunnyville Home, closer to Westwood. She was battling irreversible cancer, the kind that spreads quietly until it rages out of control. The doctors had not discovered it until her pancreas, intestines, and liver were close to surrendering. The progress (*such a strange word to use*, I thought) along its preordained path was rapid and deadly.

I needed to apologize for not believing what she told me the last time I saw her. As far as I could see, divine Providence was the last thing working in her life.

The week before, my favorite parishioner, Esther Savacini, old Radar Brain, had called me at home on my day off, sounding more indignant than usual.

"Do you know what that no-good Sonny Orr is doing? What are you going to do about it, Reverend? You know, you should be doing something to help that poor woman."

It took no effort at all to imagine the pointing finger waving under my nose. It could be as deadly as Joey's pistol.

"Esther," I said, trying to stem the flow. "What am I going to do about what?"

"He's putting Andrea into that awful place, Reverend Daniels. He just doesn't want to care for her, that's all."

I could hear her heavy breathing through the phone line as she charged on all cylinders.

"Maybe he thinks it is the best place for her, Esther."

Sonny Orr, a heavyweight hitter in the Westwood Christian Church where I served, was a thick barrel of a man who had risen to be president of the congregation at the age of forty-two. He imagined himself to be a big fish in a small pond and did whatever necessary to keep it that way. We were cordial but not what I would consider friendly. He came to church on Sundays but spent all of his time in the office counting the offering, rather than in worship.

"Andrea has no business being in that hellhole, especially way up there in Cumberland. All she wants is to die at peace in her own home." Esther's voice softened a touch. "Please, Reverend Daniels, she is going in today. Meet me there so she'll know we haven't given up on her."

The note of pleading touched me. I didn't know what good it would do, but I agreed to meet her there that afternoon. Sandy griped at my leaving the family on a day that was supposed to be reserved for us, but I didn't know how to keep everybody happy.

When I arrived at the nursing home, I walked in on a maelstrom of heated shouting and scurrying staff. Andrea Orr sat in a wheelchair outside the admissions office. A young woman in a plaid skirt and white blouse, with half glasses hanging from a neck strap, hovered solicitously while making soft reassuring noises. I guessed she was a social worker. What jolted me was the voice of the thin, cobwebby-haired creature in the wheelchair.

"Keep that fool away from me. He's no son of mine. Get me out of this dump. I ought to gouge your eyes out for this." Mrs. Orr's shrill voice echoed off the walls, her eyes showing hate and fear.

"Now, Mother, you don't mean that." Sonny stood hunched over in front of her chair, his immaculate gray suit stretched tight around his torso. He rubbed his hands together and kept glancing sideways, as though looking for an escape route.

When he saw me, he straightened up with a grunt. Turning to face me, his face showed surprise.

"Mister Daniels, I didn't expect to see you here."

Sonny liked to make a point of not acknowledging my role as pastor of *his* church.

"Your friend, Esther Savacini, called me."

Sonny winced at the mention of her name. I wondered what I might be getting myself into here. Sonny regained his smooth smile and waved his hand.

"I apologize for Mother. She's making a terrible fuss about coming here. I don't know why. We agreed that this is best for her." He turned back to the forlorn figure in the chair and continued with a sickly sweet smile, "Didn't we, Mother?"

Andrea spit on him. Sonny's face turned purple as he wiped his cheek with a silk handkerchief. I stepped forward, warily, speaking too loudly, as though she came from a foreign country.

"Mrs. Orr, hello, it's me, Reverend Daniels."

Her eyes held mine in a fierce gaze. "So, they called in the heavy artillery, eh? Why are you here? Did my mealy-mouthed Sonny-boy put you up to it?"

The bitterness in her voice hit like a slap to my face.

"No, I did, Andrea."

I never thought I would be so glad to see Esther Savacini.

"Oh, Esther, save me. Get me out of here. You understand, don't you?" Andrea's voice pleaded. Her eyes filled with tears, but none spilled over onto her cheeks. "This so-called son of mine is no better than a criminal."

"Mrs. Orr, it's time to take you back to your room," said the woman with the half glasses. She treated the tumultuous scene as an everyday occurrence, and now she patted Andrea on the shoulder.

"Keep your dirty hands off me!"

We stepped back in unison, while her sharp words echoed down the hallways. All was still.

"Let me talk to her." Esther's calm voice broke the spell.

I breathed a sigh of relief. This was like playing dodge-ball with a blindfold. I had the sense that I could get clobbered in the middle and never see it coming.

Esther pushed the chair off to the side of the lounge. I

heard low murmurs, but I couldn't make out what Esther said. I turned to Sonny, who clearly showed annoyance.

"Sonny, your mother's pretty upset."

"You think *she's* upset! Let me tell you about upset, Mister Daniels." Sonny unbuttoned his suit coat and furiously paced in front of me. "Did you see those bruises and scrapes on her cheeks and hands? Do you know how she got those?"

Without waiting for an answer, he raged on. "Twice this week I found her outside in the middle of the road on her hands and knees crawling up the street. Fortunately, it was three o'clock in the morning, so nobody saw her. I had to pick her up and carry her back to the house. She was screaming bloody murder the whole time and beating me with her fists, yelling in front of the whole world, 'Let me go! Let me go! My son hates me! Get this monster away from me!'"

Sonny stopped his pacing and checked his perfectly coiffed hair in the glass of the office door. "How do you think I felt? Well, I'll tell you. She's away from me now. This place can have her. She's too much for me and my wife to handle anymore."

He sagged inside his suit, looking exhausted by his story. I felt worn out by it.

"Don't worry, Sonny. It sounds like you did the best you could. You know, with the drugs and all, she's not in her right mind, and you mustn't be offended by what she's saying. This is probably the best place for her, so don't let it get to you."

We trailed behind the social worker pushing the wheelchair back to Andrea's new home. Before I left, Esther volunteered me to pray. Andrea lay in the bed, her back turned defiantly to us, accentuating how frail and alone she looked. Esther, mouth set in a grim line, tried to pat her on the hand. Sonny stood at the foot of the bed, foot tapping on the linoleum, glaring at his mother. My prayer sounded pitiful to my own ears. *Why did things have to be this way for Andrea, or for anybody* I wondered.

Now, a week later, I drove back to apologize to Andrea, if she would let me. I walked in the front door of the center and into the dense wall of nursing home smell. The combined odors of urine, over-cooked roast beef, and industrial strength disinfectant are recognizable the world over. I passed through the lobby full of pictures and plants into the plain, institutional yellow hallway.

I wanted to pass as quickly as possible through the maze of wheelchairs and carts parked at various angles, occupied by palsied, drooling, gray-skinned . . . I want to say children of God, but, forgive me, they looked for all the world like wispy-haired gnomes. Some were restrained by vests that had long straps tied behind their chairs and under the seats.

One old gentleman, dark gray hair growing out of his ears and nose, kept up a continual monotone of "Yep, yep, yep, yep," his head bobbing up and down to his own private beat. A woman in the middle of the hallway, both feet on the floor, pushed her chair back and forth, making shrieks like fingernails scraping a chalkboard. I tried to anticipate her next push and feinted like a fullback charging up the middle on fourth and one.

All the doorways looked the same, and I mentally kicked myself for forgetting Mrs. Orr's room number. I paused at one and looked in. In the corner sat an ancient black and white television with the flat characters of a soap opera silently mouthing their lines on a ghostly screen. The figure in the bed lay perfectly still, eyes closed, hands folded over her chest. Taking a deep breath, I stared for a minute until I saw her chest rise slightly.

I felt a soft plucking at my sleeve. I quickly turned around with a startled "What?"

A small sparrow of a woman stood there in a cotton housecoat, her watery blue eyes locked on my chest.

"Please, " she said in a whisper. "Please, take me home. Please take me home with you."

I gently pushed her hand away from my arm, murmuring, "I'm sorry. You'll have to talk to your nurse."

I continued down the hallway, hesitated, and turned around. The sparrow still stood there in the middle of the corridor, looking confused and alone. I started back toward her when a nurse stopped me.

"Can I help you, sir?"

"Oh, yes, thank you. I'm looking for Andrea Orr. I'm her pastor."

"Right in there." She pointed to the next door beyond where we stood.

"Thanks."

I took one more look down the hallway, and the aides were escorting all the residents back into their rooms for naptime. I pushed open the door to Mrs. Orr's room and stared in amazement. Andrea sat propped up on three pillows, wearing an elegant pale blue robe. I immediately noticed her six glittering rings of various sizes and value, three on each hand. Her scrapes and bruises were barely noticeable, and her hair looked brittle, but it had been pulled back and tied with an old-fashioned pink ribbon.

She studied me with frank curiosity. I wasn't sure I recognized the calm, collected woman who said in an even tone, "How do you do?"

"I'm fine. It's me, Reverend Daniels, Mrs. Orr. Do you remember? I was here the day you came to Divine Providence."

"I'm sorry, Reverend. Of course. You'll have to excuse me. It's all a little hazy," she said, brushing a stray strand of hair from her forehead. "I must look a mess."

"You look just fine. May I sit down?"

I pulled up a straight-backed chair and placed it at the side of the bed so I could face her on an equal level. "Mrs. Orr, I've come to apologize."

"Please, call me Andrea. What on earth do you have to apologize for?"

"The day you came in here I told your son not to worry, that he was doing the right thing. You . . ." I hesitated, then pushed on. "You were saying some awful things and carrying on, and I figured he must be right, that you were too much to handle." I had been leaning forward tensely as I spoke, and now I leaned back.

"You've spoken to Esther, then?" Andrea asked.

"Yes. She told me about the social worker's report. Esther is very upset with your son."

Andrea seemed not to have heard. She stared at the far wall for a long moment.

"This place is awful, Reverend. You just wouldn't believe it." She spoke in a whisper. "My roommate is totally incoherent and the staff are always too busy. I ring and ring but they don't come. It smells horrible, and the nights, they're the worst. Some of these poor souls scream all night, on and on."

She squeezed her eyes shut and turned away. "Why would he put me here? I'm the only one in this whole wing who still has my right mind. There's nobody to talk to."

I swallowed the lump in my throat. "I'll listen, Andrea."

I pulled my chair even closer. "I couldn't believe it when Esther told me that Sonny was overmedicating you. It's a good thing the center did their evaluation. I'm sorry I didn't believe you the day I was here. You must have been terrified."

Andrea turned back to look at me. "It's okay. You didn't know."

She put one hand over her eyes. "It was like I was in some long, black tunnel where I kept running and running, crying for help. Then I woke up and I was here. Margaret, that's the social worker, a lovely girl once you get to know her, told me that Sonny was giving me almost twice the prescribed dose. No wonder I was out of my mind. Thank God for Esther. She knew something was wrong."

I tried to absorb what this woman must be feeling. "What else did the social worker have to say?"

"She stopped in yesterday, while Esther was here, in fact." Andrea smiled. "Do you know that dear friend comes here every day? She drives from Westwood to Cumberland and back every afternoon. She even brought me my rings. In the week I've been here, Sonny has stopped by one time, stood there at the foot of the bed, and left as soon as he thought he could."

Andrea let out a long sigh and stared for a moment. "Where was I? Oh, yes. Margaret came in and Esther asked her about going home. Margaret said there was really no reason for me to be here. She did say, however, that I would need nurses twenty-four hours a day to monitor my medications. Right away Esther started making plans and telling her that she would look into getting the nurses and lining up friends to help out. Reverend Daniels, I get excited when I think about it, but I'm almost too afraid to hope."

"Please, call me Scott. Don't you think she can arrange it?"

"Reverend . . . Scott, let me tell you. I know what's going on with me. I'm dying. I'm sixty-one years old, and I know I am not going to see sixty-two."

I started to protest, but Andrea cut me short. "No, it's the truth. Save that for somebody who needs it, like that McCrady boy. What a shame, and his family has tried so hard with him." She shook her head. "Anyway, when the doctors opened me up three months ago, they said it was hopeless. It's spread too far and too fast. They couldn't do any . . ." Her voice broke. She swallowed, then continued. "They could not do anything." She said the words slowly, pronouncing each word distinctly.

"Scott . . . yes, that does sound better. You're too young for me to call you Reverend. Scott, do you have any children?"

"Three. Samuel, my son, is five, and Brandy is three. Then there's the baby, Susie."

"Are they at Westwood Elementary?"

"Sammy will start kindergarten in the fall. Boy, that doesn't make me feel young, believe me."

We both laughed.

"I was a kindergarten teacher at Westwood. I would have been your son's teacher if I hadn't gotten sick. I loved it, all those bright faces and their excitement. They're not bored with school yet and everything is fun. Oh my," she said with a contented sight, "those kids were my life."

This time a tear did escape. As it ran down her cheek, she began to cough. The coughing made her gasp and clutch at her abdomen.

"At least now maybe I'll get to go home," she managed between surges of pain. "Margaret says that I have a right to be there, and that there is no need for me to stay here."

The coughing stopped, leaving Andrea with a sad smile on her face. "I miss it so much. My husband and I built that home. He let me pick out whatever I wanted to buy to furnish it. And I'll be able to see Mrs. Beeges, my baby. You'll think I'm silly talking about a dog like that. Don't ask about the name. She's a German shepherd and probably weighs close to one hundred pounds. She's very protective of me. Sonny hates her because she won't listen to anybody but me."

She laughed again, then grew quiet.

The afternoon sunlight coming through the window blinds grew weaker. While I waited in the silence, I watched the little particles of dust dancing and rising like small, vulnerable ballerinas caught in the beam, only visible when in the direct light.

"It really hurts."

I glanced back at her and immediately stood up. "Do you want me to get a nurse?"

She shook her head. "No, please sit down. Stay with me, if you can. I was talking about Sonny."

"Well, you let me know if you need something. I'll be glad to stay with you." I sat down again and crossed my legs. "What did you mean about Sonny?"

"I mean I've lost him. He's no good. I know that's a terrible thing for a mother to say, but it's true. He's the only family I have left, and look at what he's done."

"Do you mean putting you here?" I asked. "Maybe he thought it was the best thing for you. Maybe he was scared or uneasy with your disease," I studied her face, then added, "and with your dying."

I feel everyone is entitled to some defense, but this only served to make Andrea angry.

"He's a miserable excuse for a son. And if you're going to sit there and take his side, you can leave right now."

She pulled herself up a little farther in the bed and gave me her best elementary school teacher frown.

"Okay, okay." I tried to make a hasty retreat. "I just thought he couldn't be all bad. I'm sure you and your husband were good parents to him."

"That's just it. Maybe we were so good to him that we ruined him. I should say, I ruined him. His father was disappointed in him, but he tried not to let it show. He did everything he could for him. No, it's my fault. He's my only child. I babied him; I gave him whatever he wanted."

She slumped down on the pillows. The pink ribbon had come undone so that her hair flew every which way. It reminded me of the dust in the sunbeam.

"He's named for his father, Charles Winston Orr, III. But that's about as close to being like his father as he'll ever be."

Andrea reached up, took the ribbon out of her hair, and began nervously wrapping and unwrapping it around her fingers.

"My husband died a little over a year ago, and I miss him so much. The pain never goes away. But you know what? Sonny never grieved for his father. I've never seen him give any sign that he missed his dad. Hand me a tissue, please."

She wiped her eyes and nose. Her story was stirring something deep inside of me, a growing uneasiness that I couldn't explain.

"It's all my fault. I gave him too much. I bought him whatever he wanted when he was little. We sent him to a good private college, and what does he do? Takes a job making pizza. Four years of college and he wanted to start his own pizza shop. He failed, of course. And he never repaid us one cent. We paid for his car, and when Sonny wanted to get married, his dad found a job for the girl in the county offices. My Charles was a county commissioner, you know. Nobody else wanted to hire her, but Charles got her into the row offices. We bought and furnished an apartment for them, and then we didn't even charge any rent. And what is he doing now? Running a video store." She gave a snort of derision. "It must be me. I don't know how to be a good mother."

"Well, if you ask me, Andrea, he's a big boy now. It's time for him to make his own decisions, suffer from his own mistakes." I'm not sure I'd like somebody saying the same to me, but I thought, *at least I understand Sonny a little better now.*

"Believe me, he's not going to suffer," Andrea said with an edge of bitterness. "When his father died, I let Sonny and his wife move into my home with me. I was lonely and needed help with Mother, who is eighty-nine."

She shook her head back and forth. "The poor dear, she has always been so terrified that she would end up in a nursing home. Well, she never will, if I have anything to say about it."

"What do you mean?"

"Sonny gets it all when I die, but what can I do? I own real estate all over this county and a couple of businesses. Charles was very good with money and did well with our investments. Now Sonny will get it all and lose it. I know he'll lose it, he's no good with money. But what can I do? There isn't anyone else I can leave it to."

"What about your mother?"

"She couldn't handle it, she's too feeble."

"Well, it's your money, Andrea. You can do whatever you want with it."

"He hasn't earned any of it. Why is he like this, Scott? I think that's what he's worried about, getting his hands on that money. He wants me declared incompetent so he can have it before I'm in the ground."

Andrea breathed heavily and I could see her hands tremble.

"Well, he can have it. He'll blow it all and then what? Who will be around to bail him out? Mommy won't be . . . around . . ." Her voice trailed off.

I put my hand on hers. She grasped it fiercely, squeezing while I winced in pain. "Reverend Daniels, do you know what I would ask God for even more than a cure for my cancer? Do you know what I want more than my own life?"

Andrea sat up, her hands a vice on mine. "That before I die, one day Sonny would come in here, put his arms around me, and say 'I love you.' That's all. He never touches me. He barely even looks at me. He has never once in his life said to me, 'Mom, I love you.' Tell me, is that too much to want? Is it too much to ask God for a son to say he loves me?"

Her words dissolved in tears as the last of the afternoon sunlight faded.

SIX

1972

"Schkat, lookee. Watch me, Schkat!"

I turned to watch Donny do a belly flopper into the pool.

"Did ya see, huh Schkat, did ya see?"

Donny pumped his fist in the air, grinning from ear to ear. The bald spot on his head reflected the afternoon sun as he jubilantly shook himself like a big, round puppy.

"Okay, boys," I called. "It's just about time to get out of the water."

My "boys" were in their twenties and thirties. Every one of them was mentally retarded and lived in a state-run institution outside Pittsburgh. I volunteered to be a counselor for one week at the day camp where the residents of the hospital could get a taste of good old summer fun. It was disconcerting to have a group of five campers with shaving stubble demonstrating the emotional level of six-year-olds.

Just then Liz, the head counselor, sauntered up to me.

She reached over and pinched the fat at the top of my trunks with a hard twist, then laughed as I tried to rub the pain away.

"I wanted to remind you about your big saxophone solo at the campfire on Friday, so don't forget to practice."

She spun on her heel and started to walk away. After a few steps she turned around and called, "Don't forget what I told you, Daniels. None of those religious songs. We don't need your kind trying to preach to these poor slobs."

Donny stayed close to my side as we walked to the bathhouse, shaking his head and muttering to himself.

"What's the matter, Donny?"

"She's not a nice lady, Schkat. She's mean to you and to my other fwiends."

I put my arm around his shoulder. "I'm glad you think of me as your friend, Donny."

"You're a nice man, Schkat. You're teaching me how to swim and make stuff with leather."

"Thanks. I'm glad you're having fun at camp, but don't they teach you stuff like that at the hospital?"

He put his arm around my waist, completely unselfconscious about giving affection, and gave me a sly look.

"Wanna know a secret?"

"Sure, what's your secret?"

He pulled me off the path and into the shade of a maple tree.

"I'm going to get married." He reached into his rolled-up towel and took out the wallet he had crafted earlier in the week. Reverently he opened it to show me a picture of a girl of about twenty, her face showing the obvious features of Down's syndrome.

"This is Cindy. She's my girl. She's nice, not like that mean Liz."

"She's very pretty."

"Youbetcha! My mom says I can come home from the hospital and live with her again, so I told Cindy I would get her out, too."

"Does your mom know about that?"

"No, it has to be a secret, Schkat." Donny's face grew serious. "My mom gets real nervous sometimes and I don't want to get her upset. She might make me go back to the hospital if she finds out."

Donny put his hands on my shoulder. "You won't tell, will you, Schkat?"

"No, Donny. I promise. But how will you take care of a wife?"

He beamed. "I have a job. I go on the bus every day, all by myself, to the sheltered workshop. We put stickas on stuff for stores and put nuts on big bolts. That's my favorite. I feel like a big man then."

I rubbed his bald spot. "You are a big man, Donny. Don't let anybody tell you different."

At home that evening, after supper, I excused myself and went upstairs. I stood in the hallway and listened for a moment to be sure my mother remained in the kitchen doing the dishes. Satisfied, I carefully opened the door to the big walk-in closet where we stored winter clothes and Christmas decorations. I snapped on the light and pushed my way through the heavy coats.

In the back sat a large trunk. After listening once more for any footsteps, I gently lifted the lid. The top layer was white tissue paper. I carefully placed it on the floor to one side. Underneath lay a black robe and beside it a worn case with gold-rimmed glasses and a dog-eared Bible. I stroked the soft robe, touched the glasses case, and then picked up the Bible.

The pages crinkled as I opened it up at a place marked with some pages of manuscript. It was my father's sermon, the one he was preaching when he died. He always wrote the scripture reference at the top of the first page. There, in his handwriting, I read "Romans 8:18-27." In my secret ritual I never read the pages, just looked at them and remembered.

After carefully putting everything back in its proper place, I went back downstairs.

"Mom? Could I invite one of the guys in my group of campers to come over for dinner some time?"

She stopped wiping the sinks for a moment. "Scott, I have enough trouble trying to keep you fed, let alone adding another mouth to feed. And I don't know what I'll do if you don't slow down yourself. I can't keep buying you bigger and bigger clothes."

I swallowed my embarrassment at the reference to my expanding waistline. Maybe it was a bad idea anyway.

The next day Donny didn't get off the old green school bus from the state hospital. Chester Peters, his best friend, told me that Donny was not allowed to come. Chester didn't know why. He only knew that Donny had thrown a fit at the hospital the night before. He threw some chairs and hit one of the aides.

JOHN TUFT

"He got a shot," said Chester, knowingly. "They make you all fuzzy and sleepy. Donny hates the shots. Everybody hates the shots."

That evening I persuaded Mom to let me take the car, and I drove out to the hospital, bewildered at the change in Donny. In the few days that I had been around him he remained calm, kind, and cooperative. He called me his friend.

Decades of steel mills had turned the brick of the imposing structure a dingy brown. The grim-faced nurse at first did not want to let me see Donny—something about behavior restrictions. I explained who I was, that Donny had been doing so well, and that I wanted to let him know I was thinking of him.

She looked me up and down, shrugged her shoulders, and said, "Maybe you can talk some sense into him."

She led me down bleak corridors to a locked room. Inside I saw a cot bolted to the floor, no blanket or sheets on the mattress, and nothing else in the way of furnishings. A despondent-looking Donny sat on the bed in his stocking feet. The nurse left us alone.

"Donny?"

He looked up and stared at me with glassy eyes. A day's growth of beard covered his chin. I remembered his joy at the pool yesterday, but his face registered despair in this dingy room.

"Donny, it's me, Scott. I missed you today."

Still no response, so I went over to sit on the bed beside him. We sat quietly for a while.

"They took my wallet, Schkat."

His voice sounded gravelly, like he had a sore throat.

"Who took your wallet?"

Donny put his head on my shoulder and cried. I patted his back until the tears slowed.

"What is it Donny? What happened?"

"My mother . . . ," he choked out between loud sniffs, "asked was it okay if I stayed here. She changed her mind. She can't take care of me and could I stay here a little while more."

56

"I'm sorry, Donny. I know you wanted to go home."

"I'm a man, Schkat. I can ride the bus by myself. But I love my mom, so I said okay. I'll stay here for a little while."

"But what happened to your wallet? You said somebody took it." I had a sinking feeling in my stomach.

"I told my mom I was going to get married and I showed her my picture of Cindy. The nurse heard me and came over. She said I was being crazy. She took my wallet and I got mad and I threw things and hit my mom. That's when they gave me the shot."

I didn't know what to say.

"Now they have my Cindy and they say I will never go home. I don't want to live, Schkat, I don't want to live." He curled up on the bed and sobbed.

After a while I said, "I'll play a song for you at the campfire, okay Donny?"

He didn't answer.

The next night I went to the equipment storage barn at the camp. I took out my saxophone to practice. I liked playing alone because I could forget everything else and let the music speak, capture me, drive me deeper and deeper.

I walked around high up in the loft as I played, my music beseeching the stars above, twinkling beyond the open window. I thought of a night years before when a dream of mine had been shattered. In a storm, I had locked myself up in a prison. I played for Donny, who didn't have a choice, as he watched his dream being ripped from him. The last echoes rang out as I played for Donny alone in that room.

I didn't go to the campfire that night. I couldn't face the thought of spending the evening with Liz and my rowdy fellow-counselors, or enduring their constant teasing and sarcastic remarks. Donny's place would be empty. I figured I'd already played him my best song there in that old shed.

SEVEN

The present time

I took roll call of my best friends gathered around me. A king-sized bag of M&M's, a bottle of Coca-Cola, two glazed donuts from the Davis sisters' bakery, and an issue of *Sports Illustrated* sat in a semicircle on my desk in the church office. I noticed as I reached for the candy that my hand still bore the red marks where Andrea Orr had squeezed it. I stopped it in midair and looked at the imprints, remembering our visit yesterday.

Deciding I could snack later, I stood up and went out the door into the sanctuary. The simple, high-ceilinged room consisted of light blue walls, blond wood in the pews, and a large cross hanging on the wall behind the communion table. On each side of the room three stained glass windows, designed and installed one hundred years ago, filtered light through colored glass with charming, wavy imperfections. Sometimes in the afternoon I liked to watch the watery images and, in the stillness, say my prayers for the people of my congregation.

I went to the back row and sat staring at the chancel. The cloudy day made the room dark and gloomy, and I felt a little creepy. Being disciplined in prayer is not one of my strong points, but I tried to picture the different members in their regular pews.

Halfway back my eyes came to the spot where Connie sat each Sunday. Something came to mind, but not a prayer. Sandy and I were rarely on the same wavelength anymore, but Connie, in my mind, promised all the warmth and caring that I longed for. Again, I pictured her at the back door of her house that night, allowing myself to fantasize about her unbuttoning the next button of her blouse.

"You're terrible, Scott," I muttered aloud.

"Talking to yourself, Preacher Boy?"

I jumped up, smashing my shin on the back of the seat in front of me.

Zeke laughed. "Saying your prayers?"

"I—I didn't hear you come in, Zeke." I rubbed my leg, the image of Connie wiped from my mind.

"So I gathered."

He took a step toward me, and I could smell the alcohol on his breath. His greasy hair complemented the yellowish, bloodshot whites of his eyes. The damaged side of his mouth twitched, and he rubbed it with the back of his hand.

"I don't get to church much. Don't get me wrong, I believe in God, but churches and I don't get along. Too many hypocrites for my taste."

I watched him as he took a few steps down the aisle, wondering what brought him here. He gazed at the cross, then turned back to me.

"People think I'm crazy. I don't know, maybe I am."

"Do you want to go in my office and sit down, Zeke?" I started toward the door off to the right of the chancel. He hesitated, then followed me into the room and took a seat in front of my desk.

"Know why I quit going? Because of Penny." Zeke shook his head in disgust.

"Who's Penny?"

"She was just a mutt, not a hunting dog or anything like that. Best friend I ever had. That dog was loyal and she went everywhere with me." Zeke lowered his eyes to the floor.

"What happened to her?" I asked.

"Same thing that's going to happen to me. Old age caught up with her. Did you ever have to watch someone you love die, Preacher?" He looked at me with teary eyes.

I flashed back to a bright, sterile hospital room, lost for a moment in long ago pain. I pushed it aside to concentrate on Zeke's story.

"Me and Penny did everything together. She followed me into the bars, on my walks to feed the squirrels and redbirds, to the grocery store. Everybody understood about me and Penny. We were friends. She didn't judge me or condemn me, and I didn't expect her to be perfect. She didn't stare at my face, she always stayed close, she never lied to me, and I could trust her. She was a true friend, Preacher Boy, always there for me."

Zeke took a tattered handkerchief out of the pocket of his stained pants and noisily blew his nose.

"I need a drink. Got any money, Reverend? It'll just be a loan, I promise. I'm cutting down on my whiskey, tapering off. I know it's no good for me, but I gotta taper down so it won't kill me. A couple of quarters would sure help."

"I don't think so, Zeke."

"Well, maybe later, huh? Anyways, I asked my old preacher if I could bring Penny into church with me. She wouldn't cause any trouble, just lie there under the pew. I guess she could probably sing better than some of those old windbags. But they told me no, dogs weren't allowed to be in church. It would disrupt the proceedings. What on earth are they doing having proceedings in God's house? I ask you, do you think that's fair? Do you think God cares if a dog is in church, especially considering what else he has to watch go on in his name?"

I started sputtering something noncommittal, relieved to see Zeke getting out of the chair.

"Can I ask you something else, Preacher Boy?" He made no move toward the door, just fidgeted with my books that lined the walls.

"Yeah, I guess so," I answered warily, wondering if he was back to wanting money. "If you'll stop calling me Preacher Boy."

He laughed, which made him start coughing. He coughed so hard I thought he might keel over. When he regained his breath, I asked him if he was all right.

"Sure, sure, I just need that drink real bad, that's all. I call you Preacher Boy cause that's what you are, and until you prove otherwise, that's what you'll stay."

"I don't like it," I said defensively.

Zeke shrugged. "You don't know yet, do you, whether you're really grown up or just pretending? And you don't know if being the minister of the Westwood Highandmighty Christian Church makes you high and mighty or just a fool, right?"

The man could certainly keep me off guard. He didn't wait for me to answer, thankfully.

"It's Billy. I want to know if you can save Billy."

He stared at me. I noticed for the first time that the undamaged side of his face had a handsomeness to it, a dignity that even the ravages of his drinking did not entirely mask. I blinked a few times, searching for the appropriate response.

"Save Billy from what?"

"From me. Billy don't hold much truck with me, and I can't say as I blame him. I'm not much of a father, but that don't mean I don't love my boy." Zeke pulled at the front of his shirt with both hands. "I don't want to see him end up like me, do you understand?"

"What about you don't you like?" It was what they taught us to say at seminary in Pastoral Care and Counseling 101.

Zeke voiced his contempt. "And you wonder why I call you Preacher Boy? What kind of dumb question is that? Do *you* like me? Do you want to *be* like me?"

Without stopping for breath, he pressed on. "I used to be the top engineer at the paper mill. When some of those young college hotshots got stuck, who do you think they always called on?" His voice rose in volume. "Me, that's right. I was good, very good. Now people hate me. They cross the street when they see me coming, telling their kids to stay away from that bad man."

His last words bounced off the walls and ceiling. Now, he pleaded, "Please, help my boy. He has nothing to live up to, so he's dying, dying inside, and I can't reach him. He's going to lose his dreams and his wife, and then his own little boy is going to hate him. And all I can do is watch."

Zeke leaned across the desk, his face inches from mine, his voice drilling right through me. "If you really are a man of God, save my Billy."

Later, as I drove up Horse Rock Mountain toward home, Zeke's pleas kept echoing in my head. How could I know what to do for Billy when I didn't even know what to do for me?

Instead of turning right onto Horse Rock Road, I turned left and drove to Connie's house.

She had supper started when I knocked on the back door.

"Come in, Scott. See, I remembered this time to call you Scott."

The warmth of her smile and the coziness of the kitchen made me feel like I had come to the right place. Connie's sweater and tight jeans served to heighten that feeling.

"Is there something you needed to see me about?" she asked as she stirred potatoes in the frying pan.

"No, not really. I just felt like seeing a friendly face." I returned the smile.

"Has it been a rough day?" She came and sat down across the table, pushing a steaming mug of coffee in front of me.

I looked at her for a moment, noticing the gold flecks in her hazel eyes catching the light. "Sometimes I think it's more than I can handle, helping people through some of the worst times in their lives. I don't think I'm cut out for it because I never feel like I'm doing any good."

"From what I can see you're pretty good at it, Scott. I feel very comfortable talking to you, like you're listening to every word I say, caring about me and not just going through some checklist in your head of right things to say. You don't give people a lot of empty God-talk either."

Those eyes captivated me and I hoped that I wasn't too obvious. I could sense an aura of danger in the back of my mind, but keeping it back there only made me feel more excited. *Here is somebody who understands me and what I go through,* I told myself. *I deserve that much at least.*

"Is there something wrong? You keep staring at me," Connie said.

"Oh, I'm sorry. I was just thinking . . . uh, about . . ." I could feel the temperature rising in my cheeks. It was like I was watching some stranger taking over my body and doing things I never thought I would do. How far would I go in playing with fire like this? Until I got burned?

"Is something wrong, Scott? You seem preoccupied."

"No, nothing's wrong. I . . . well, I never felt so relaxed talking with somebody before. I could stay here all night."

Connie laughed. "Oh, you could?"

"I'm sorry, that didn't come out right. I mean, I like being with you. There's no pressure. You don't beat around the bush, or make demands, like . . ." I bit my tongue.

"Like the church? Or like your wife?" She studied me until I squirmed. "Is there some trouble between you and Sandy?"

I fidgeted with my mug, sliding it back and forth on the table.

"It's okay, Scott. You're allowed to be human." Connie's voice softened.

I felt like I might cry. "Why are you being so nice to me?"

"Now, that's a strange question. You sound suspicious. Listen, I put up with the likes of Billy ever since we were in high school. Now you come along and treat me like a decent human being. It's nice, let me tell you. You don't have to pretend with me about anything. Some people think ministers don't have needs like the rest of us. I don't agree with them. I've noticed lately that you seem burdened down with cares or worries or whatever, and I'm glad you think enough of me to share them. Scott, you're only human, get that through your thick head." She went back to the stove and put pork chops in the grease.

"You're making me hungry," I said.

"I should be sending you on home, Scott." She came over

to me and pulled me up out of the chair. "But I'm not sure I want to."

I touched her on the cheek, hoping my heart would not drill a hole in my chest with its pounding. She lightly kissed my fingers, and this time I did reach out to hold her.

"You must think I'm terrible," she murmured into my chest.

"Likewise," I whispered.

She pushed away. "I've got to call Mikey in for supper. Thanks for being here."

I stood, legs shaking, trying to will her to step back into my arms. "No. Thank you. Thanks for understanding and caring."

"I'll be here whenever you want to stop again," she said lightly, and then she called Mikey.

Arriving home a few minutes later, I was in another world until I opened the garage door. In the back corner, opposite the door into the house, sat Billy's paintings. The eyes of that doe looked at me without blinking. The eyes held me with their unearthly quality that was made all the more jarring by the tear in the canvas.

"Daddy's home!" Sammy burst out the door, followed closely by his little sister, Brandy.

"How's my Zoobilee Zoo gang?" I swept them both up in my arms and squeezed until they squealed.

"Scott? Is that you? Where on earth have you been?" The anger in Sandy's voice contrasted sharply with the joy in the children's.

"What's wrong?" I asked as I came through the door, all innocence and light.

"Don't tell me you forgot." Her scornful voice trailed off from the hallway leading back to the bedrooms at the other end of the house.

I didn't remember, so I said so. "I don't remember."

She came back into the kitchen pulling on her jacket. "Now there's a big news flash. Why am I the last person you think of, Scott? Why does everybody else come first with you except me?"

"Sandy, come on. What did I forget? You know it takes a lot out of me to try to help people. You could at least ask me about it once in a while."

"Oh, you poor baby. Try putting up with three fussy kids all day. I need some help and some attention, too, you know." She put her hands on her hips. "Is it too much to ask for you to come home so I can go get my hair done? It's not a big deal like your precious job, but I don't have a whole lot else to look forward to, or to keep me from going completely crazy."

Our fights were usually a lot quieter and sulkier than this. In fact, usually they were silent tests of will. This real outburst broke all the established rules of engagement.

"Calm down, Honey. We can talk about this later." Actually, her wrath frightened me. I didn't want to talk about it; I wanted it to go away. "I'll make it up to you, I promise. Please don't yell at me anymore."

She shook her head in disgust. "I don't know how else to get your attention, Scott. Remember how it took you six years to get through seminary? You kept quitting and taking other jobs that made you unhappy. So you'd quit them and go back to school and start the whole circle over again."

I've never been proud of my record. Her words hit below the belt.

"Yeah, I remember. Of course I do."

"Now don't start pouting on me, I'm serious. I should have spoken up then, but I kept my mouth shut. I figured you needed to straighten it all out for yourself. But then the kids started arriving and you still couldn't make up your mind. I've always tried to do what's best for you, but I'll tell you, it's getting pretty lonely for me, Scott."

Her eyes brimmed with tears, but she was too mad to let me wipe them away. She brushed my hand away and headed for the door.

"Can you still make your appointment?" I asked, feeling a big hole opening up in my gut.

"No, Mister Concern, it's long gone. But I'm going out for a little bit anyway. I need to get some fresh air and talk to some grown-ups." With that she was gone.

"Daddy?" Brandy tugged on my pant leg, looking sad.

"Yes, Pumpkin?"

"Do you and Mommy need some happy juice?"

When she first learned to talk, apple juice came out happy juice. The name stuck as a family joke.

"I don't know what we need, Honey. Don't worry, everything will be fine." I hoped I sounded more convinced than I felt.

I gave the kids balogna sandwiches for supper and kept them amused until bedtime. While they took their bath, I got the baby fed and ready for bed. After an exhaustingly interminable bedtime routine with Sammy and Brandy, I sat down to rock the baby in the big rocking chair. Before I knew it, I fell asleep.

The dream came back. First came that awful blackness. Then I turned my head, and there were the windows. The white mist infiltrated the tiny spaces around the window frames, working at them until the windows soundlessly opened outward. The swirling fog came billowing through this time, rushing toward where I lay rooted to the bed. A voice came out of the mist. It sounded like Connie.

"All I want is for you to come through that door and tell me that you love me. Is that too much to ask?"

EIGHT

"Did old man Zeke put you up to this?" Billy looked over at me with a wry grin. "If anybody needs to be saved, it's him."

We were driving up Backbone Mountain early on a Monday morning, my day off, on our way to the last thing I ever expected to be doing. We were going hunting.

"Who said anything about saving you? Or Zeke, for that matter?" I glanced apprehensively toward the back of the pickup, where two bows and a bunch of arrows lay on a pile of blankets and old tarps.

"I'm not stupid, Preacher. I know my old man came to see you and he probably asked for some money, right? Then a few days later you come traipsing around work, asking if I could show you what it's like to hunt in these mountains."

"Maybe I'm just trying to fit in here," I said defensively. "Maybe I'm just trying to do my job. If I remember right, you invited me that night Joey shot himself. Anyway, how do you know about Zeke coming to see me, and what business is it of yours what he might or might not have said?" I didn't like being caught redhanded.

"Relax, Preacher, I came didn't I? Are you really in the business of saving people? It's gotta be a tough line of work, especially since most people don't want to be saved." He shook his head, a knowing smile on his face.

"No, I'm not dumb enough to think I can save anybody, Billy. I have enough trouble handling my own life. I try to give people hope, a little bit of hope. And I try to let them know that somebody cares about them."

"Like who?"

"Me, I try to show them that I care. I figure that way they might listen when I tell them that God cares."

"That doesn't sound like any cakewalk of a job, either, Preacher."

"I would really prefer that you call me Scott." I wondered if he would ask me about that night at the American Legion and the blow-up over the paintings.

"Why?" He took his eyes off the road and looked at me with raised eyebrows.

"You get right to the point, don't you?" I didn't know why I began to feel more nervous than I felt already about our little expedition.

"Preacher and Reverend are titles that you earned, they show respect. Don't you want that? It's what you are, isn't it?"

"Well, yeah."

"You don't seem real sure, Preacher."

"I'm not sure of a lot of things, Billy. Like what I'm doing riding up Backbone Mountain at six in the morning with a fluorescent orange hat on my head, sitting beside a guy who makes me wonder if I have any idea why I'm a minister." Oddly enough, I found myself liking this man with the desperado mustache.

"You think we're all crazy, don't you?" Billy laughed at his own question.

"No, I don't think that. I think maybe I'm crazy for heading into the woods to freeze who knows what body parts off and put an arrow through some poor tree's heart, while the animals die laughing."

Billy chuckled as he turned off the main road onto a bumpy gravel lane pitted with chuckholes. Our conversation stopped while we hung on to the door handles to keep our heads from crashing through the roof.

Every bone in my body rattled, and I expected to take my teeth home in my pocket.

After a few miles Billy steered the truck up a steep track that ended in a meadow. I looked around, puzzled, until I recognized it as the one from his painting.

"Let's get started," Billy said, climbing out of the cab.

I groaned and moaned as I clamored out, marveling at how someone could consider this fun.

"Just stake me to the ground and let the ants eat me," I protested.

"Now remember what I told you," cautioned Billy. "You head west toward the Savage River, follow it down for a couple of miles, then circle back up here."

"Shouldn't we go together?" I asked, looking around anxiously.

"The best way to experience these woods and mountains is on your own. Besides, I'll be just a mile or two away, so don't worry. I showed you how to use the bow, and from what I saw, you don't have to worry about dragging a carcass back up here." He laughed.

"Thanks a lot." I held the bow gingerly.

"I'll give you a couple of hours. And remember, the weather can change pretty quick up this high. If you see something coming, turn around and get back to the truck pronto."

"Just don't forget about me."

He gave me a pat on the back and pointed west. "If you see any bears, just stand still until they pass."

"Bears?!" I sputtered. "You didn't say anything about bears."

But he was already gone, melting into the trees so quickly he might have been a ghost.

"Well," I sighed, picking up my bow and arrows, and awkwardly slinging them over my shoulder. "Hi ho, hi ho, it's off to work we go."

After fifteen minutes of thrashing through the underbrush and being scratched by vindictive thorn bushes, I still hadn't come to anything resembling a river.

"Who does he think I am, Daniel Boone?" I grumbled.

I tried a little farther to my right and was rewarded with the sound of rushing water. The Savage River turned out to be a glorified stream, running through a six-foot gorge that held more rocks and boulders than water from what I could see.

"That doesn't look too savage to me," I said confidently, slipping and sliding down the steep bank.

The water looked clear and clean, inviting a rookie hunter to have a drink. As I leaned over to dip my cupped hand into the swift water, the bow swung around and gave me a rude slap in the face.

"Ouch! Why didn't somebody warn me hunting was dangerous. I'm glad it's not a gun."

I straightened up and did my best Indian scout impression, surveying the lay of the land while balancing on two slime-covered boulders. All I could see were more rocks and muddy banks, and beyond them the stately trees, which watched me impassively, mutely.

"Maybe I can just follow the river for a while," I said to the trees. "Maybe I shouldn't be talking to myself so much, either."

I laughed, and the sound of it echoing in the gorge along with the song of the water gave me pause. I laughed again, louder. Next I screamed and hollered, waving my hands in the air while dancing a crazy jig.

"I am Conan, King of the Hunters," I bellowed. The trees ignored me.

I started jumping from one rock to another, whooping and singing, the bow and quiver of arrows flopping against my back. I tried one last mighty leap for the far bank. I missed. My foot slipped between two wet stones, twisted horrendously, and became lodged. I fell on my back in the water, stuck, and strangling on the bowstring and quiver strap.

I flopped helplessly for several minutes, tugging at my pant leg and trying to yank the bow off my back at the same time. My impression of a beached whale only got me soaking wet and my foot more firmly trapped. The icy water chilled to the bone in no time.

"At least it will keep my ankle numb," I chattered. "Along with everything else."

I managed to get untangled from my weapons and awkwardly tossed them toward the bank. They bounced off the rocks and were swept downstream.

"Great. What else can go wrong?" I muttered.

At that moment it thundered.

"Why don't you just send hail and locusts now!" I shouted at the sky.

I sat in the freezing water, trying to stay calm and take stock of my situation. Billy did not expect to see me for two hours. I was sitting in a mind-numbingly cold bath, unable to get out. My ankle throbbed. The first drops of rain were starting to land on my face. And, oh yes, if any bears did happen along, I had thrown my only defense downstream. Hunting is fun.

Then it dawned on me why the river was in a mini gorge with smooth sides. The rain grew harder. The river bed was one of its main courses down the mountain. As if to confirm my worst fears, I noticed that the water had risen over my pants in the last fifteen minutes. It would work its chilly way up my torso, to my neck, and then . . .

I screamed. "Billy! Billy, help!"

The wind started to blow, more thunder boomed, the rain poured, and the river ran faster. I kept screaming at the top of my lungs until I grew hoarse. I glared at my watch, hoping my acute attention to it would make the hands move faster. The water rose above my bellybutton.

I tried praying. "God, help me. I don't want to die. Please, help me."

When the water reached my chest, I started thrashing, frantically pulling on my leg, screaming in pain and terror. I turned into a wild man, throwing handfuls of gravel and mud from the river bottom at my twisted foot. I began crying hysterically.

Then a vision of a dark angel came splashing toward me from upstream. Billy's black hair was matted to his head by the rain and his face was grim and determined. But when he reached me, something strange happened.

I screamed, "Help me!" and in desperation reached for

his arms. He froze. His eyes took on a faraway look, a glassy-eyed stare of dread and dismay. He started to shake, violently, and took a step backward.

"Billy!" This couldn't be happening. "Billy!"

He remained transfixed. I picked up some pebbles and threw them in his face. Slowly he came out of it, shaking his head as if to clear it of some evil picture.

"It's okay, Preacher. I'm here." His voice sounded strained.

He immediately went to my foot and worked it loose. Grabbing me under the arms, he pulled me out of the river. We struggled up the bank, gasping for a few moments at the top until he made me get up and keep going.

"We've got to get you warm right away."

Leaning on his shoulder, I hopped and limped through the trees to the truck. Billy fished a camouflage tarp and some rope out of the back and told me to wait in the truck until he returned. I laid on the seat, shivering like crazy, certain I would never be warm again.

Billy opened the truck door about twenty minutes later. "Come on, let's get you warm."

We hobbled back under the trees. Billy had rigged the tarp to make a lean-to, and a small fire burned under its shelter. After settling down on the jacket he spread on the ground, I asked him, "Where did you learn to make a fire with wet wood in the middle of a rainstorm?"

"I was a Ranger," he replied perfunctorily.

"You were a forest ranger?" I asked in amazement.

"No."

I was puzzled. "What other kind is there?"

"Army. It's something like Special Forces."

"Were you in Vietnam?"

"Yes. How's your foot?"

"It's kind of stiff now." My curiosity was aroused. "I thought you said you started college."

"That was later. At nineteen I was hiding in the jungles

of Southeast Asia, trying to stay alive. Get closer to the fire. You need to get as warm as you can."

"But what did you do?"

"Listen, Preacher, it's not a subject that I appreciate talking about. I don't mean to be unkind, but it's really none of your business."

"I'm sorry, you're right." I studied the fire. "Thanks for saving me back there." I motioned in the direction of the river.

He looked embarrassed. "I guess I owe you an explanation. But promise me," he pointed his finger at my chest, his eyes flashing, "that you won't ever tell anybody."

The intensity of his tone took me by surprise. "I—I promise. Thanks for trusting me, Billy."

He simply stared at me for a long minute, until I squirmed closer to the fire and poked it with a stick. He turned his attention to the sparks that flew upward, and that distant, glazed-over stare returned to his eyes. I waited. The sound of the rain, the smoke from the fire, and the danger of the narrow escape combined to cast a spell on both of us.

"I was nineteen." Billy's voice came in a whisper. He looked out at the dripping trees as he told his story.

"Ranger school was exciting. We were in the woods and mountains most of the time. I learned about nighttime scouting, survival, tracking . . ." he paused. "Other stuff, like using a knife, or a wire, to kill silently."

For a time the only sounds were the water on the leaves and the tarp, the soft crackling of the fire. Billy kept rubbing his mouth and mustache over and over. He stared into the gloom as he continued.

"Nothing prepares you for the real thing. I was a kid and I thought it would be exciting. I never thought about feeling somebody's last breath on my cheek while I strangled him. We operated in the Delta area, mostly at night. One night my squad surrounded a village where we suspected the Viet Cong took shelter. Somebody started shooting."

Billy's eyes filled with the same fear and dread I had seen at the river. His voice became husky.

"I burst into a hut with my pistol and knife, our weapons for close quarters fighting. There was a movement in the shadows. I fired into the darkness and heard a scream. When I got a light I found a kid, just a kid of ten or so, defending five or six other younger kids with an old pistol. I had shot him in the gut. I picked him up and held him while he died."

Billy started to tremble. "It was his eyes. They were so big and so scared." His words came out in a tortuous gasp. "They kept asking me why, why? And then, in a second, they were empty. I can't ever get those eyes out of my head. I put them in that painting of the doe. Those are his eyes, that kid, staring at me while he died."

Billy's chest heaved. "Back there at the river, for a moment I saw that boy with those eyes, asking me, 'Why? Don't let me die.'"

Billy threw his head back and let the rain beat on it. "Tell me, how do you get saved from something like that, Preacher?"

He spun around and walked off into the trees, his shoulders shaking, while I watched the smoke curl up toward the weeping heavens.

NINE

"Is this really how we want our church to be led?"

Sonny Orr rubbed his hands together as he warmed up to his subject. My throbbing ankle made it difficult to keep my mind on the matter at hand, namely, the monthly meeting of the board of elders of the Westwood Christian Church. My responsibilities included moderating the meeting, which usually amounted to trying to get other opinions heard besides Sonny's.

"What are you talking about, Sonny?" Esther Savacini chimed in right on cue.

"I'm talking about the behavior of our so-called minister, Mister Daniels here." He gestured theatrically toward me.

I came fully awake. This smelled like a set-up, and Sonny sounded confident that he had enough ammunition for an ambush. I looked around the table, wondering if anyone else knew what was coming, and if they did, why they had not warned me. Of the twelve people sitting there, none would look me in the eye.

Uh-oh.

"It seems to me," Sonny paused to clear his throat and consult a paper in front of him, "that our minister has a strange way of tending the flock, as it were."

He slowly went around the table, looking at each person for a brief moment, letting them know he was in full control and making sure he had their full attention.

"First, there is the matter of his being at the scene when Joey McCrady had his unfortunate accident."

"Accident?" I leaned forward in disbelief. "That was no accident, believe me."

"Then you admit that you were there?" Sonny smiled smugly as he sprung the trap.

"What's so terrible about being there? I didn't shoot him.

He shot himself. I got a call in the middle of the night to come down to the American Legion and see if I could talk some sense into him." I didn't see how Sonny could make a major case out of an emergency call to help someone in distress.

"And who called you to that . . ." Sonny looked disdainful as he uttered the word, "cheap bar?"

"Billy Simpson, but what does that have to do with anything?"

Several people rolled their eyes and exchanged knowing looks. Esther made soft clucking sounds.

"Everybody knows he's no good, just like his father. How Connie ever got herself mixed up with him, I'll never understand," Esther prattled at her condescending best.

"And who were you with when you allegedly almost drowned and hurt your ankle?" Sonny pressed his case like a prosecuting attorney.

"What does that have to do with this? And there is no 'allegedly' about it, Sonny. Just ask Billy."

"So," declared Sonny, triumphantly, "Billy Simpson was at this incident as well." He looked around the table, then lowered his voice to a conspiratorial whisper. "And was there any . . . alcohol consumed on this little hunting trip?"

"Sonny, this is preposterous!" I exploded. "Why don't you just say what you want to say and get it over with. I nearly died out there in that river and I owe my life to Billy."

A picture flashed in my mind momentarily of Billy leaning over me in that raging water, his eyes seeing another horror, his mind struggling with dark terror.

Sonny took advantage of my silence to jump back on the attack. His voice oozed sweet reasonableness, but what he said made me want to vault over the table and tear his eyes out.

"I only meant that maybe Billy's problem is taking up too much of your time. I understand your wife hangs around in the bars over in Cumberland now, drinking until she is intoxicated. Maybe you should be more concerned with her and this congregation than with some lost, worthless soul. Who's just like his father, I might add."

I saw purple, then red, then black with yellow stars. "You arrogant . . ." Somehow I stopped myself, breathing deeply, trying to stay in control of myself. "It's none of your business, but if you insist on bringing it up, one night my wife did need to get out of the house after being cooped up with the kids all day. She went over to Cumberland, had one drink, and came home."

At least that's what she told me. Sonny's seed of doubt worked its way into my mind even as I defended Sandy. She normally didn't drink at all, but she was under a lot of strain lately. *What else had she done that night* I wondered.

"Whatever you say, Mister Daniels. It seems to me, however, that, like I said, you need to be paying attention to your own family rather than meddling in other people's."

"Sonny," I felt weary, my mind in a turmoil. "What are you getting at now? It's getting late and we need to wrap up this meeting so we can all go home."

"Well, Mister Daniels, I think I deserve a fair hearing, don't you?"

"A fair hearing on what, Sonny?"

"On your interfering with my mother." Sonny brought his hand down on the table with a loud bang that made us all jump. "What gives you the right to tell my mother that she should be able to be in my house when she is such a sick woman? What gives you the right to give my mother encouragement when I'm the one who has to give up my life to try and keep her from crawling down the road like an animal in the middle of the night?"

He didn't wait for an answer but spread his hands out and continued plaintively, "I'm a simple man. You all know me. I run a video store, my wife is a clerk, we live a simple life, and we work hard for all that we have. My whole life is in this town and this church."

Sonny's voice started to quaver as I sat there in disbelief. "We won't ever be able to have children, so when Mother's gone I'll be all alone, but I have to do what I think is best for her. This man," he pointed at me, his voice breaking, "is ruining my family, my home. Who knows? Maybe next he'll want to take my church away from me."

With that he got up and walked out of the room. I looked to Esther for support, but she only shrugged her shoulders. I felt like the man on the moon as I closed the meeting. The others avoided me while they filed out, leaving me alone with Esther.

"Don't worry, Reverend," she said. "Andrea is getting out tomorrow, and then she'll be home where she wants to be. Imagine him, calling it his house already."

She left before I had a chance to raise any question about her lack of support in the face of Sonny's attack. I collected my things, my blood boiling, and went out to the car. I opened the door and flung my papers on the seat, then I slammed it closed. It felt good, so I opened the door and slammed it again, and again. I pulled it open for one more.

"Feel better?"

I stopped in mid-slam. "Hello, Zeke." In my annoyance at Sonny I didn't even care that I had been caught acting childish.

"Did that door talk back one too many times?" In the light of the streetlamp Zeke's smile looked like a leer.

"I wish it had. Then I might feel better."

"Bad day with the highandmighty?" Zeke stepped out of the light and shambled over, bringing with him the usual odor.

I leaned against the car and sighed. "Zeke, what am I doing here? I don't seem to be getting anywhere."

"Where are you supposed to be getting?"

"I don't know. I always thought I should be making some kind of difference to people as a minister. Instead, I feel like I'm nothing but a glorified babysitter."

"What does your Boss say?"

Too caught up in my own misery, I missed Zeke's meaning and kept talking. "When I left seminary they told me I had everything I needed to be a helping professional, that I could counsel, give support, plan programs, lead worship, comfort people through the worst times, and wear the academic hood with pride. I had made it, I was one of the chosen, I belonged up there with lawyers, doctors, engineers, and all those who get initiated into professions."

Zeke studied me. "Is the real world getting to you?"

"I don't know what to do, Zeke. I feel lost in the real world. Sonny Orr just crammed all his complaints down my throat and nobody stood up for me at all. They had to know that most of what he said wasn't even true."

"Sounds like you're getting a taste of what your Boss went through."

"Huh?"

"Never mind, Preacher Boy. Have you got any money on you? I'm tapped out."

I reached into my pocket and gave him all my change. I didn't feel like taking on the whole world's problems after that session with the board. Zeke looked surprised but quickly took the money and shoved it deep into his jacket.

"I wanted to know if you would pray for somebody, Preacher Boy. His name is Rocky. He's one of my buddies and he tends the bar over at Fat Eddie's. The doc thinks he has liver cancer and won't make it. I thought maybe you could put in a good word for him with your Boss."

"Sure, Zeke, I won't forget. You say his name is Rocky?"

"Yeah. He's been real good to me. He always let Penny come in and sleep under the bar until I was done. He doesn't deserve this . . ." Zeke's words were cut off by a bad spell of coughing. "Gotta get that drink, Preacher Boy. Thanks for the money."

"Don't mention it."

Zeke started to walk away, then turned around. "You know, I think everybody's looking for the same thing, Preacher Boy."

"What's that?" I asked.

"Peace, purpose, and place. Everybody, even you, is looking for peace, purpose, and place. We could use a few less helping professionals and a few more who can show us the way to those three. Oh, and by the way, thanks for trying with Billy."

He turned back toward Fat Eddie's and walked into the night, leaving me alone to ponder his words. Zeke and Billy were becoming more and more a part of my life, but not of each other's, I mused. I guessed they wanted peace, purpose, and place, too.

As I got into the car, however, it was Sonny's words that returned to taunt me. The man was crazy, I decided. His mother wants his love, and he wants his mother's money, come hell or high water. What a world.

Then I thought of Sandy. Had she told me everything about that night? Why should she? I didn't tell her everything about what I did out here while I was "helping." When she had come home that night, she still acted grumpy and cold toward me. Did she find somebody else's shoulder to cry on at the bar?

"Stop it, you idiot," I said to the rearview mirror. Still, I wondered. The clock on the dashboard read 9:30. Maybe it wouldn't be too late to stop and see Connie.

"What a nice surprise."

Any doubts I had had melted away in the light of Connie's welcoming eyes. Too tired and upset to listen to my conscience any more tonight, I figured tender loving care offered the best balm and I could worry about the consequences later. I wouldn't be here, I rationalized, if Sandy would just take the time to try to understand my needs.

"Do you have any more of that coffee and a warm shoulder to cry on?" I made myself sound facetious, like I was not as desperate as I felt.

"Sure, to both." Connie said. "Another bad meeting? Don't let those people get you down, Scott."

"Let's talk about you; I'm too disgusted to talk about me right now." I settled into a kitchen chair, wondering at the strange, nostalgic sensation that it was *my* chair and that it had been waiting for me to come back.

"What about me? I'm not used to anybody wanting to hear about me, Scott. Thanks, though." Connie's smile drove away the last of the doubts.

"Tell me about your job, what you dream about doing in your life, your family—you know, anything like that. I want to know more about you." I wanted to pretend she was mine, pushing Billy out of my mind, pushing Sandy, Westwood Highandmighty Christian, and common sense far beyond reach.

"Why are you so interested in me?" She poured the coffee and headed for the living room. "Come on," she called over her shoulder, "let's get comfortable in here."

"Comfortable" brought all sorts of images to mind. I knew I was playing with fire, and I didn't care. If the world was going to be against me, I might as well get what pleasure I could from anyone willing to offer it. It was easier than facing the struggle at home, and besides, I told myself, if Sonny was right, Sandy was not exactly without blame either.

"The cat got your tongue?" Connie teased me as I wandered absentmindedly into the living room after her.

"Huh? No, sorry, I'm still trying to figure out what happened tonight at the meeting. Sonny Orr made some wild accusations about me, that I hang around with the wrong sorts of people . . ." I stopped, realizing the subject had turned to Billy. Maybe I needed to change topics. But for some reason I was reluctant to tell her the other image nagging at me: Andrea and our conversation in the nursing home, her pitiful dying wish.

"Go on, Scott. You can tell me." She patted the cushion next to her on the couch.

I sat down, basking in the scent of Emeraude. She put her hand lightly on my arm.

"Am I making you nervous?" she asked.

"No, I'm fine, Connie. Go on, you were going to tell me about you."

"Okay, if you insist. There's really not much to tell. I'm just a simple girl from the hills. My daddy worked all his life in the paper mill as a maintenance man, doing all the dirty jobs. My momma raised us kids, took us to church, made sure we did our chores and looked after each other. I've worked ever since I was thirteen, packing groceries or cleaning people's houses. Now I work at the flower shop, but I have my own dreams." She looked shyly at the floor.

"What are your dreams?" I prompted. The simplicity of her summation and her dreams captivated me, made me want her all the more.

"You'll laugh. I mean here you are with all your college and seminary degrees, and all your fancy books, standing up there on Sundays talking about what's right and wrong, how to make things better and help people, and here's me down at the bottom of the ladder wondering what's it like to have the whole world in front of you like that."

I took her hand in mine, softly stroking the backs of her fingers. "Dreams are important. They give us hope, and hope gives us strength for the tough times." I got the nagging feeling that I had heard my father say that sometime, somewhere. I certainly didn't need him intruding on this dubious grab at happiness.

"I never thought of it that way before, Scott. See what I mean, you know how to get through to people, make them think about what's important. I'm honored that you like being with me." She snuggled closer.

"You were telling me about your dream."

"Promise you won't laugh?"

"I promise."

"I want to go to the Cumberland Beauty Academy and learn how to be a beautician. Then I want to open my own shop and be my own boss. It may not sound like much, but I think it would be the greatest. I could have my shop downtown with all the other stores and be one of the business people. When they have Chamber of Commerce meetings I could go to those, too. Mrs. Owens is getting ready to retire, and I asked at the bank how much it would take to buy her shop down by the red light."

"What did they say?"

"They said $30,000, but it may as well be a million. I've tried to save some money, but Billy didn't help out much with the bills around here, so I've had to use everything I have to keep Mikey and me fed and clothed."

"Don't give up so easily. You didn't keep everything together this far by giving up. You strike me as somebody who hangs in there and keeps pushing. There's probably some government help for small businesses or something like that. Hang on to your dream. It's a good one and you can do it."

"Thanks, Scott." Connie looked at me, putting one hand on my cheek and turning my face to hers. "You're the first person to believe in me and to think I can do more with my life. I've been so lonely all these years, and now you come along and I feel like I can take on the world."

She pulled me to her and I didn't resist her kiss. Her lips tasted slightly salty and my heart jumped. She ran her fingernails over the back of my neck.

"I want you," she whispered into my ear.

I began to unbutton her blouse, while kissing her neck.

"You're beautiful," I said hoarsely.

"You've done so much for me, Scott, now let me do something for you. I know you need someone to trust, someone to release you from all the worries and cares. Let it be me, Scott."

I lay back on the couch with my eyes closed. This was it, the moment we'd been heading for all along. This time I had no intention of stopping.

Just then, the phone rang.

Connie pushed away from me, muttering, "I'd better see who it is."

"I'll be right here waiting." The moment was rapidly losing its golden glow, and I desperately wanted to recapture it.

Connie said hello and stood listening for a minute, her face growing more concerned as the conversation went on.

She hung up without saying another word and came back to the couch, buttoning up her blouse.

"What is it, Connie? What's wrong? Who was that on the phone?"

"It was the police chief," she said in a dazed tone. "He thought I might want to know. Billy's in jail."

TEN

"My parents are all huffy puffy with each other. They think I don't know they can't stand each other, but you'd have to be blind not to see it. I don't know why they even stay together."

The speaker was Shelley, a sixteen-year-old from Tennessee. Her soft drawl charmed me, along with the smile that revealed gleaming orthodontic wires. She talked a mile a minute, barely pausing to take a breath between stories of her parents' awful marriage and her own struggle to fit in at the new school.

We were sitting in the Pittsburgh East End Cooperative Counseling Ministry and Community Center. For one of my courses in seminary I was to spend ten hours a week working with the clients at the center, applying what I learned in the classroom to the real world. Shelley was about to immerse me in the hard realities of that world.

"I never wanted to move to this stupid place. I know I shouldn't, but I keep talking back to my momma and daddy, giving them a hard time. They act like they couldn't care less what it's like for me, leaving all my friends and my boyfriend, Chucky. They say we were getting way too serious and it's good for me to be away from him. What am I going to do, Mister Daniels?"

There was a long pause before she added, "I'm carrying Chucky's baby."

"Do your parents know?"

"Shoot no, you think I'm crazy?" Shelley twirled a lock of hair around one finger—she was the essence of sweet sixteen.

"You need to tell them, Shelley."

"My dad will kill me, Mister Daniels. You don't know

him, he's real religious. He doesn't even like me going to dances, let alone thinking about me and Chucky going all the way." She rocks back and forth in the chair, her eyes beseeching me for an answer.

"What about your mother? Won't she understand, or at least want to do what's best for you, Shelley?"

"Momma does whatever Daddy says. Look at her, having a baby last year, fifteen years after I was born. I know it's because she's trying to make things better between her and Daddy."

"Maybe it would help if I talk to them."

I saw her eyes flood with relief as she grasped at the hope that she was not alone in her crisis. I, on the other hand, had no idea what I would say.

"I don't want to be big and clumsy for the next nine months. All the kids at school will be laughing at me and all the guys will think I'm easy. I just didn't want Chucky to forget about me and think I don't love him. Now I'll be home throwing up instead of going to the prom."

I tried to think of the right thing to say, but I couldn't get past how young she looked and how she expected me to have the answer right at my fingertips. After all, I was nearly twice her age, I'd made it through college, and now I had convinced my church, my advisors, and myself that I was called to be a minister. I heard no angel whispering in my ear as Shelley popped her gum and checked her make-up in the mirror.

"How did it go today?" Sandy asked me later in our tiny apartment in East McKeesport.

"I don't know which is worse, a sixteen-year-old who's pregnant and afraid to tell her parents, or my professors who've been attacking everything I believe in from the day I started seminary." I collapsed onto the worn-out couch that we'd collected along with other hand-me-down furniture.

"You knew it would be tough, Honey." Sandy came over and rubbed my shoulders.

"Tough, yeah, but I didn't expect humiliation. And I can't get Shelley out of my mind."

"What humiliation, Scott? What happened at school?" Sandy sat down beside me on the couch.

"I wasn't going to tell you about it. I didn't want you to worry and get all upset."

Sandy had her usual reaction, exasperation with my unwillingness to confide in her. "Scott, what is your problem? We're husband and wife, remember? Why are you always so afraid I'm going to yell at you or make you feel foolish?"

I felt myself sinking further into the soft cushions, the fear creeping into my gut as it always did. I didn't know how to explain it to her, how to convey the sense of worthlessness that colored my thoughts and feelings as I struggled with the certainty that I was pretending, playing at being a man of faith, a friend of a God who is laughing at me in my feeble attempts to make sense out of my life.

"I'm sorry," she said. "I don't mean to get on you like that, but I don't think you believe enough in yourself. You have a lot to offer. You're smart and caring, yet you're always tiptoeing along, afraid of your own shadow."

She was right. Fear was a big part of my life. It was a constant companion, closer to me than my fantasies or my prayers. And for good reason, I believed.

"It's Professor Randall, if you must know. He asked each of us to tell the class about why we're in seminary. I didn't want to. You know I don't like to talk in front of a group of people, and I couldn't see that it was any of his business anyway."

"What did you tell him, Scott?"

"I just told him the truth: that I didn't know for sure why I was there. That one day in church a couple of years ago we heard that missionary who works in Ethiopia give a talk. She had just been expelled from the country, along with all the Christian workers, by the new Marxist government. Before she left, the Christians there asked her to tell the church in this country about their plight and to please send Bibles. That as long as they had Bibles to keep them connected to God they could endure. Then after church, remember Sandy, what we did?"

"Sure I remember, Scott. We both felt moved by her message and those Christians probably facing death, and all they asked for were our prayers and some Bibles. You said, 'Let's give her our money,' and we did."

We both laughed. "We thought it was a lot of money," I said.

"Hey, it was. It was all we had. We were just married, in our first apartment, couldn't even afford a decent car, and here we were giving away the last of our wedding money, $500, to help those people."

"I remember how happy we felt that day, Sandy. Not long after that I enrolled here at Pittsburgh Seminary because I felt that giving the money wasn't enough, that my dad would have said, 'Put your mouth where your money is,' or something like that."

We sat in silence for a while, absorbing the impact of the turn our life had taken that day.

"Professor Randall jumped all over missionaries when I got done telling my story," I continued finally. "He launched into a big lecture on how missionaries stomped all over the cultures, oppressed the people, encouraged exploitation, and spread disease and racism. Then he told us that liberation theology would set things straight there, get rid of the terrible consequences of, as he said so sarcastically, 'spreading the gospel of white wealth with your precious Bibles, Mister Daniels.'"

A week later Shelley and her whole family trooped into the office. Mr. Cooper had retired from the military as a master sergeant and come north looking for work in a steel mill. Unfortunately, the steel industry had just begun its nose dive and jobs were increasingly scarce.

Mr. Cooper stood about five feet six, wore his hair in a military style, and brooked no nonsense. His wife came up to his chest, walked a few steps behind him, and looked tired way beyond her forty-two years. Shelley took a chair at the opposite corner from them and stared sullenly at the walls.

"Father Daniels, please talk some sense into my foolish daughter's head," Mr. Cooper began immediately.

"Uh, excuse me, sir, but I'm not a priest or even a minister. I'm a student at the seminary."

Mr. Cooper cut me off. "Whatever, you're a man of God. Now tell her that abortion is murder and that God will send her and the baby to hell if she goes through with it."

"Mr. Cooper, I'm not here to take sides. I'm here to help all of you figure out what's best for Shelley." I wanted desperately for some angel to walk through the door and straighten out this mess. It was beyond me, that much I knew.

"Tell him, Martha," Mr. Cooper said as he nudged his wife none too gently. "Tell him about when you found out you were pregnant last year after all this time. We never even considered abortion, even though it meant a lot of changes in our lives, a lot of sacrifice, a lot of hassle we didn't need at the time. Then this . . ." He gestured toward Shelley with a look of contempt. "This whore of a daughter gets herself knocked up and doesn't want to face up to her responsibilities. We certainly didn't raise her that way. She gets that from being here in this godless city. Go on, tell him, Martha."

I looked at her with sympathy. She was a trapped animal. "Mrs. Cooper, what are your thoughts about all this? Would you support Shelley in whatever she decides to do?"

She looked from me to Shelley to her husband.

"It's okay, Mrs. Cooper. You can say whatever is on your mind in here. This is the place and the time to be completely honest about what you feel."

She cast another nervous glance at her husband before she spoke. Her voice was so quiet I had to lean forward to catch what she was saying.

"I think," she pronounced the words so distinctly that I wondered if it were the first time anybody had asked her for her own opinion. "I think it's a hard choice. I have friends who are foster parents for babies waiting for adoption and who have seen what girls like Shelley go through. It's a lot of pain and wondering if they are doing the right thing or not."

She looked at Shelley and then back to her husband. "George doesn't know this, but I have also talked to girls who have had abortions. They tell me about the pain and the terrible hollow feeling that they have, sometimes years afterwards. The hardest part, they say, is that no one thinks they should grieve what they have lost. That it's no big deal. But it's real. It's a real loss, a real pain. I just don't know, Shelley. I just don't know."

I looked at her with new wonder and respect. Maybe Shelley had an ally after all, I thought. Still, it took an hour of emotional wrangling and wrestling to make any progress. Dad just could not believe that his little girl would do this to him. Shelley didn't want to stick out at school and lose her chance at winning Chucky back.

Finally we agreed that everybody in the family would listen to all sides. They would talk to adoption people and abortion providers. They would listen without judgment and ask all of their questions. The final decision would be Shelley's, and whatever it was they would all be supportive and pull together.

"Why do you insist, Mr. Daniels, on hanging on to these quaint and antiquated notions?"

Professor Randall was on the attack again.

"It was a simple assignment," he pressed ahead. "You were to identify the places in this passage in Mark where an editor has clearly taken some oral tradition that might have grown up around a possible saying of Jesus and show how he has twisted the words to his own political agenda. Give up your old Sunday school religion, Mr. Daniels. If there ever was a real Jesus, he is long gone and far removed from your pitiful attempts to defend him. These are myths. Get that through your head."

He turned to address the whole class, reveling in his superior knowledge and our pathetic ignorance.

"People, it's time to grow up. There are no anchors in this world. The only goodness is the little bit of God that we all carry around inside of ourselves. Your job is to help others allow the God in them to be free, to discover themselves, to be what they want to be and can be. For some that will mean getting rid of this awful picture of a God of judgment and anger, or of little angels sitting on the shoulders of those who wrote the Bible dictating the words of God into their ears."

The class laughed while my ears burned.

About a week later Shelley sat across from me, alone this time.

"I have something to tell you," she said. "Can you guess what it is?"

She had just asked for a glass of water in order to take an antibiotic capsule, so it wasn't hard to guess.

"You decided to end the pregnancy."

She looked at her lap for a long moment, uncharacteristically silent. She nodded her head and whispered a soft yes.

I expected tears but none came. They came to my eyes, though, as she told me the story.

"My momma and daddy hardly speak to me now. I had to ask a friend of the family to take me. She lectured me the whole way over to the clinic. My daddy said it was wrong and wouldn't let Momma go along or help me in any way. Chucky came up to visit and he went along, but he sat clear on the other side of the waiting room. Said he met some girl named Duffy and he really likes her and would I mind if he dates her now."

Shelley ran her hands over her belly. "It hurt a lot more than I thought it would. I didn't really want to do it. I kept waiting for my momma to tell me no, not to do it. I called my best friend in Tennessee so she could tell me not to do it, but she wasn't home. Later that night I went to my room and cried and cried—I couldn't stop. I know it was loud enough for them to hear, but my momma and daddy never came to check on me. The only thing Momma said was, 'Shelley, what are you going to do when you get to heaven and your baby comes up to you and asks why did you kill me, Mommy?' I couldn't believe my momma would say that, but she did."

Shelley stood up and looked at herself in the mirror. "I guess this is what it feels like to be on my own. It's a big hollow feeling that will swallow me up and I'll just disappear. Momma won't even let me hold her new baby anymore."

I sat there stunned. Shelley told me she guessed she wouldn't need to see me anymore.

I stood up and held out my arms. She clung to me fiercely for half a minute. Then she quietly left.

Still without tears.

I sat in the library letting my mind wander. *I want to be a great preacher, but I'm afraid. I want to be a great leader of people, inspire them to great heights, but I am lost. I keep reading about great people like John F. Kennedy and Martin Luther King, Jr., or Henry Ward Beecher, and how they had numerous affairs with other women even though they were married. If I am great, will I get to do the same?*

I reached into my briefcase. There was my dad's Bible. I didn't dare let Professor Randall see it. I wondered why I hung onto it, and I wondered if I had helped Shelley find that little bit of God—enough to set her free.

I put my head in my hands. I had no anchor. Faith in the goodness of people was an illusion. My "greatness" was mocked by memories of camp and my humiliation at Eddie's hands all those years ago. Fleetingly I saw Donny and foolishly hoped that he wasn't still in that bare little room getting those shots.

I took the Bible out, transported back by the smell of the old leather of my father's most prized possession. I withdrew the sheets of his sermon script and began to read it. The story he was telling that morning drew me in. I was looking for something—hope, courage, I wasn't sure exactly what—but it was the first time I ever read the pages, and the words—his words—became my talisman against the crowding despair:

Once upon a time there was a kingdom ruled by a kind and good king who had a castle surrounded by vast and beautiful gardens which stretched for miles in all directions. The king had special people who helped him take care of his gardens. The people were honored to do it and devoted their lives to keeping them looking beautiful and ready for the king to visit.

The gardeners never knew when the king was going to come to their part of the garden. That meant they always kept the gardens looking neat and beautiful. The king let them live in the gardens, and they were allowed to enjoy them all they wanted, as if they owned the gardens themselves. All he asked was that they tend them, keeping them ready.

There was a gardener who had two sons. He was proud to serve the king, and he was proud of his two sons. As they grew up, the sons begged their father to let them have their own part of the garden to care for. But he always told them they would have to wait until they could handle the responsibility. It was hard work, and even though the king had not been around for what seemed forever, they still had to keep the gardens ready.

The sons begged and begged, insisting that they were ready because they wanted a chance to serve the king, too. Finally the father gave in and allowed them each to have a little part way back in the farthest corners, far, far from the castle and even farther away from the main gardens. He told them that they would be in complete charge of their small plots. They had to keep prepared for the king's visits. It was their responsibility, and it would be their full-time job now. If others needed help with their patch of land, the sons would be expected to pitch in like any other gardener.

The first son started out with good intentions. He was going to work hard and keep his part of the garden looking beautiful and productive. But after a while he started to grow tired of working the demanding soil. It was hard, and he wanted to do other things. Eventually, he paid less and less attention to his plot, seeking other diversions. The ground soon became overgrown with weeds.

The first son told himself that he had tried but that it seemed hopeless waiting for a king who never showed up. Besides, he figured he would have plenty of warning before His Majesty showed up to rush about and get his garden presentable. Anyway, it would be more exciting and rewarding to whip the plot into shape on the spur of the moment, knowing somebody would finally reward him for his efforts.

Now, the second son received the smallest plot of land back in the farthest corner of the garden. No one ever went back that far. It was a long, hard trip. Some said it was dangerous. But the second son was humbled to have a chance to work in the king's gardens; it didn't matter to him where it was. He worked long and hard, slowly getting his plot to the point where it was beautiful and produced exotic flowers and good fruit.

Day after day the son worked in the garden, with no one ever coming to see the results. But he was thankful to serve in his place in his own way. Happily, he looked forward to having his lord visit. Others told him that the king had never been known to come that far into the gardens, but the son didn't seem to mind. He was happy and ready.

One day, years after the father had given his sons their own plots, His Majesty finally arrived unannounced, leaving no time for last-minute corrections or adjustments. When he came to the first son's garden, the king's eyes grew wide in amazement and disappointment. The garden was in shambles. One could hardly tell it had ever been productive land.

The king was grieved as he looked at the weeds and fruitless trees. There were some who said it was the king himself who had planted the gardens years ago, and anyone who saw his disturbed eyes that day believed it was so. He called the first son to him and asked in a quiet but stern voice, "What have you done to my garden?"

The son squirmed under that royal gaze. Finally he could only stammer, "I—I—I tried sir, but you never came."

"I'm here now," said the king, "and you are not ready. Therefore you must leave my garden."

The son left, shaking his head and muttering, a disgrace to his father and his king.

Then the king went into the garden of the second son. His

Majesty smiled as he saw all the beautiful, well-cared-for plants. He went over and touched the shoulder of the son who was kneeling, digging around some flowers. The son, startled, seeing who it was, said, "I'm sorry that I have nothing to give you, my lord, in honor of your visit."

"You have done all that I asked," said the king. "You have given me your service with your whole heart. What other gift could I want?"

The son replied, "Then I am thankful that you have come to the garden. Enjoy it, I have kept it for you."

The king smiled and said, "Give the first son's garden to this worthy son, and he will have charge of both. It is his duty."

And it was so.

I reached the end of the sermon, puzzled by the sudden ending. Maybe I hadn't picked up all the pieces of paper that day. I turned the last one over and saw scribbled there in my father's handwriting, "for son—my prayer" and the reference Romans 8:18-27.

I found a Bible and looked it up, which only left me more confused. The reference had nothing to do with the story and vice versa. I knew the story was vintage Reverend Daniels, the *real* Reverend Daniels. Service without self-pity, duty without doubt, that was my dad. But what was that note supposed to mean? Had my father been thinking about me the morning he died? What did he want to say to me? What was his prayer for me?

In my mind I saw that intensive care unit and his struggle with the ferocious pain. He couldn't have been thinking about anything then. I saw myself lean over the bed again, trying to say the words, while silently cursing my mother's cowardice. I wanted desperately to know. What was my father's prayer for me?

ELEVEN

The present time
I think I spend half of my life in the car. Usually I have the radio on, sometimes to fill up the silence and hide my thoughts from myself. At other times the music entertains, helping me to keep on going without going crazy.

The day after the phone call at Connie's, I drove the twenty miles to the Allegany County Jail in Cumberland in silence. The silence left me no place to hide. My thoughts, my conscience, my fantasies screamed at me for the entire drive without words, without sound, without letup.

"What am I doing here?" I finally asked my reflection in the rearview mirror. I despaired of finding an answer.

First, I had come so near to being with another woman, and it excited me, knowing that she wanted to be with me, to touch me, to revel in the delicious wickedness of it all with me. For once I could get what I wanted. For once, I, Scott Daniels, would not wimp out but go full-speed ahead to grab some of life's pleasure for myself. With Connie I didn't have to worry about being Mister Prim and Proper, or pretend that I didn't want to devour her body with all the passion I kept locked away in some moldy cavern deep within myself. She could be mine, all mine. I could do whatever I wanted. I could have whatever I wanted. She didn't seem worried about guilt, so why should I?

On the other hand, my memories haunted me. Why couldn't I forget them, or at least ignore them, emasculate their power so that I could have some peace? After all, I was just a kid at camp. For that matter, I was hardly more than a kid when my dad died.

Zeke's words about peace, purpose, and place came back to me. I knew it was wrong to be trying to have an affair with Connie. I knew it was wrong to keep justifying my actions with a "but I deserve a little happiness" rationale. Why didn't I care more about the wrongness of it, though? That bothered me as much as the actions themselves. Did I want to prove that I could do it, that nobody could tame me? Or was it my insecurities that made me want to put my head down on her shoulder and cry, to feel her stroking my hair and telling me everything would be okay?

"You're hopeless," I said to the man in the mirror.

"God," I spoke to the mountains that framed the horizon on both sides of the road, "the only prayer I can think of is to tell you that I'm hopeless. But I guess you already know that."

As if to prove it, I let my mind return to the picture of Connie, laying back on the couch, trying to see in my mind's eye what should have happened next in that magical moment. The images quickly dissolved as I remembered the rest of our conversation before I left her house.

"Billy's in jail?" I asked, astounded "For what? What did the police chief say he did?"

"He's been accused of burglary. Chief Keller said some woman over in Keyser filed a complaint. Apparently she and Billy went home together from a bar and after he'd gone she said she discovered several of her belongings were missing."

"What kind of belongings?"

"A pair of earrings, her watch, some money." Connie got up to find her cigarettes. "I know Billy, and he's no thief."

"No, you're right. There's got to be some explanation." I watched her pace around the living room, taking deep drags and blowing smoke angrily at the ceiling.

"I can't believe this bugs me like it does," Connie blurted out as she smashed the cigarette butt into an ashtray.

"Why shouldn't it bother you, Connie? It's probably some kind of a mix-up."

"No, no, it's not that." She sat down across from me. "I keep thinking about him being with another woman. I don't know what I expected him to be doing, but hearing somebody say something about Billy and another woman just got to me."

I felt my stomach give a lurch. Here I had been plotting

to make her all mine and she was still expressing feelings for Billy.

"You and I weren't exactly acting like a couple of angels ourselves, were we, Scott?" She gave a short laugh. "I guess what's good for the goose, or whatever."

She didn't say it in a mean voice, but suddenly I felt uneasy.

"Aw, Scott, don't look so shocked. We knew what we were doing." Her voice sounded affectionate as she continued. "What's that old hound dog gotten himself into now, I wonder. Scott, will you go see him tomorrow and tell him I'm worried about him? It would mean a lot to me."

I started to say something, then closed my mouth, no longer certain where I, the Reverend Scott Hypocrite Daniels, fit in.

"Scott?"

"Yeah, sure, I'll go see him and tell him what you said."

She came over and gave me a long kiss. "I'd say give him that from me too, but the other prisoners might wonder about the two of you."

The memory of her laughter at this joke echoed through my brain as I found a parking space on the street below the jail. Her concern for Billy was eating at me. If she still cared for him, why was she willing to be with me? Why was I, a married minister, wanting her to be all mine? I am hopeless, I decided disgustedly.

The county jail sat on top of a hill, next to the courthouse. I parked at the bottom and began the long trek up to the top, wishing I had a donut for energy. Signs directed me around to the back of the courthouse and down dingy stairs to glass doors. My hands shook as I drew a deep breath and walked into the foyer. I'd never been in a prison before, and I questioned why I was walking into one now. *Was it for Billy, for Connie, or for my own sake?*

Directly in front of me loomed a door made of iron bars. "Yep, it's a prison," I thought to myself. I wondered if they made that loud clang like in the movies when someone shut them. To my right, overflowing trash cans complemented the battered chairs set beneath signs that covered the walls: "NO SPITTING," "NO SMOKING," "NO PACKAGES," "NO ALCOHOL," and "NO TOUCHING."

I looked to my left. A sliding glass window, slightly open, revealed a room with three desks and two huge, brown-uniformed sheriff's deputies. A third man in blue jeans with no belt, a white T-shirt with a pack of cigarettes rolled up in one sleeve, and shoes without laces swept the floor while exchanging raunchy jokes with the guards.

I stood there, unsure of what to do. Timidly, I knocked on the glass. No one turned around. I considered leaving and making my excuses to Connie, but had second thoughts about it when I recalled Billy's actions for me that day on the mountain.

A walkie-talkie beeped and sputtered on the desk nearest to the window. One of the deputies turned around to switch it off and spotted me.

"Can I help you?" he barked in a drill sergeant voice.

"Yes, can I see Billy Simpson?"

"What? I can't hear you. Open the window."

I obediently pushed on the glass, which gave a loud shriek as it moved three inches and then stuck fast. I pushed on it some more, but it was no use. It wouldn't budge. I awkwardly wedged my face into the small opening, cleared my throat, and tried again.

"I wanted to know if I could see Billy Simpson. If not, it's okay."

"Are you family?" The other guard spoke, while the third man stopped sweeping to stare at me.

"No, I'm his minister. He belongs, er, well, his wife belongs to my church in Westwood and she asked if I would come see Billy." My cheeks felt numb in the tight space, and my voice sounded like I had marbles in my mouth.

The first guard gave me a quizzical look, then shrugged his shoulders. "Yeah, I guess it's all right."

The other one yelled, "Come over to the door, Preacher, and I'll let you in."

The man with the broom snickered and made some comment that I couldn't hear. The deputy laughed and said, "Well, he'll soon find out," as he crossed over to the door.

I stepped over to the bars and waited. In a moment the deputy appeared with a large ring of keys dancing and clanging in his hand. He unlocked the door and swung it open, but put out a hand to stop me after I took one step through the opening.

"I'm sorry, but I have to search all visitors. We had some guys try to break out last week, so for now all visitors get searched."

I held my arms out from my sides, expecting to be frisked the way I had seen it done on TV.

"Uh, Preacher, no, I mean a strip search. I ain't never seen you before, so I don't know you from Adam. If you will step into this room here, please." He indicated a gray-green door with a small window made of wire-reinforced glass.

I followed him through the doorway into a room no bigger than a janitor's closet, my heart in my throat. Surely this guy would give me some privacy. Wrong.

"Please undress and hand me each item of clothing." His impersonal tone made my skin crawl.

I unbuttoned my shirt and handed it over. The man felt the collar and around all the other seams. I couldn't believe this was happening.

"Your shoes, please." They were thumped and poked.

"And your pants."

I had heard ominous things about strip searches. My hands shook as I unfastened my pants and handed them over, terribly self-conscious about the white roll of fat lapping over the elastic of my underpants. I could feel my face burning as the guard looked in all the pockets and felt the crotch. *Please, not the underpants.*

"Okay, Preacher. That's enough. You can get dressed while I go get Billy. I'll bring him to the conference room where the prisoners meet with their lawyers. Sorry, but it's all we got. We don't get many visits from men of the cloth."

I dressed as rapidly as possible, my cheeks still hot, picturing the other guard and prisoner laughing at my discomfort. I peeked out the door before stepping into the deserted hallway. I spied the door marked CONFERENCE and hurried across to it, feeling exposed every step of the way. The floor was littered with cigarette butts and smelled worse than a junior high locker room. From somewhere in the bowels of the building I heard shouting and banging.

"Here he is. Take as long as you want, Preacher."

I turned around. Just inside the door stood Billy. He looked like he hadn't slept, and his disheveled hair and wrinkled clothes added to the hollow fatigue in his eyes. One eye had a nasty-looking black and blue goose egg underneath. He didn't say a word but stared at me.

"Billy." I couldn't think of what to say. He continued to stare at me. For a moment I had a crazy notion that he knew about Connie and me. "Why don't you sit down?"

Billy shrugged and ambled over to one of the chairs. The silence grew while I studied my hands, trying to pin a thought down long enough to form a sentence.

Finally I laughed nervously and said, "They strip searched me so I could get in here."

"I doubt it was as thorough as the one I got when I came in last night." Billy's voice sounded distant.

"What happened to your eye?"

"Some of the boys in here got the mistaken opinion that I was in here for abusing my kid, so they tried to administer some jailhouse justice." He shrugged indifferently. "I set them straight."

This hard-edged Billy was a stranger to me. His emotionless tone and flat demeanor had a menacing quality to it that made me very uneasy.

I fidgeted with my fingers. "I guess you know how to take care of yourself, huh?"

"How's Connie? And Mikey, is he okay?" His face softened for a moment.

"Yeah, they're fine, Billy. Don't worry about them. Let's get this straightened out."

"Look after them, will you, Preacher?"

His request had a note of finality to it that I decided to ignore.

"Billy, what happened last night?"

He sighed and ran his fingers through his hair. "I met this woman at the Keyser Korral. She kept coming on to me, but I wasn't interested. Well, she got so drunk she couldn't even stand up straight. There wasn't anybody else to see that she got home safe, so I took her."

Billy stood up and paced the small room, shaking his head. "Why don't I ever learn? I got some coffee into her and we got to talking. Soon as she found out I was Zeke Simpson's son, her whole attitude changed. All of a sudden I was a pariah, lower than scum. She couldn't get me out of there fast enough. I wasn't more than two miles down the road before the police pulled me over."

I was dumbstruck. "Surely the police can see through that, Billy!"

"I'm Zeke-the-No-Good's kid, remember? Case closed."

"Maybe if I talked to them, gave you a character reference or something."

"Preacher, no offense, but you're from the outside. Even the blood of the lamb like from those old hymns doesn't wipe out family bloodlines. You've got a father, don't you? Well, you've got his blood, too. It doesn't go away when you become a man, and in a place like these hills around here, it decides who you are, no matter what you wanted to become."

"So you're going to go to jail because of that? What about the truth? What about justice?"

Billy laughed. "What about Mom and apple pie?" He turned serious again. "I'm locked in, Preacher. I'm locked into Zeke's blood just as sure as I'm locked up in these iron bars.

I'm not saying I like it, but I do understand it. Don't worry, everything will work out okay."

It was my turn to shake my head in bewilderment. "What about your paintings? Are you saying your talents, your gifts, are an aberration, and you're supposed to be a loser and keep the balance of nature intact here in this little corner of the world by sacrificing them and letting the forces of hopelessness push you around however they want to?"

I threw up my arms in despair. "I can't accept that. You're better than that. I know you are. I still have those paintings at home. They didn't come from Zeke-the-No-Good. They came from a man with a soul, a man with a spirit that rises above this place."

"Look, Preacher, you've done your job. You came to see me, and I appreciate it, more than you know. Now go home to your family and quit worrying about everybody else's life. We all take chances in life and we all make choices. I'll deal with mine. Why don't you deal with yours?"

He went back out the door before I could respond. I wanted to run after him and pound some sense into him. I wasn't about to let my father's blood rule my life, even if it meant breaking every prescription and iota of his dogma and gospel. Billy could carry his own private prison around if he wanted to, but I planned to break out of mine one way or another.

Billy remained on my mind as I wrestled with my sermon for that Sunday. I told myself it was my calling, not my father's. His words were not mine, his aloofness and distance were not mine, and whatever doubts and emptiness Dad might have felt were not mine either. I wouldn't let them be. Well, maybe I couldn't be as sure of that as I might like to think. Doubts and emptiness might explain my own behavior lately. But I didn't want to think about that.

I've always shared my own struggles—up to a point—with my congregation, maybe to a fault. I didn't want to be on anybody's pedestal. My dad's church treated him like he was next to God, except when it came time to give him a raise.

Being held up that high can put an awful lot of pressure on a guy like my dad whose main concern was to do God's business whatever the cost. The effect on the rest of his family could be equally disorienting. Did we live with Dad or the Reverend Daniels?

I spent the rest of the week thinking about losers. It's a dominant theme in my life—with girls, when it comes to sticking up for myself, being a leader, being a son, being a husband, inspiring others to faith—in all of them I qualified as a loser. Being a loser is like being in jail.

On Sunday I stood in front of the assembled congregation, a gathering of the high and the low, the weak and the mighty of Westwood Christian Church, and spoke from the heart. I looked at their expectant faces, wanting to scream out at them, "I don't get it, so don't worry if you don't either. I don't expect much from me, so you don't need to expect much of yourselves any longer either. I'm not sure I'm doing the best that I can do, so don't get excited if you're doing less than your best. I don't have a prayer to hang my hat on and I'm running on empty, so don't expect me to fill your cup anytime soon. Go on home. We'll do this another day."

The phone lines would certainly light up all over the county if I let myself go and laid it out for them like that, I thought, as I cast my gaze over the blank faces. "The truth is for losers," I muttered under my breath.

I gathered my papers together and began:

As a child, I was what is referred to as "chubby." In addition to being painfully shy, I was overweight, and to this day I shudder in my embarrassment at wearing clothes with the "husky" label on them. It was as if my whole life centered on those extra pounds of flesh. I figured that was all people saw of me—my ring around the middle, my overgrown love handles.

I was teased about it by my family and by some I considered to be friends. There were always the well-meaning ladies in the church who would pat me on the head, or worse yet, on my stomach, clucking about my being so "healthy looking."

It was all very humiliating. I never let myself get close to anyone, although that is what I wanted most in my life: to be close to someone, someone who would simply accept me and care about me just as I was.

Yet I was afraid of being teased because it stung the most. I tried to be the best little boy that I could be, very quiet, extremely polite, wanting to please . . . and very lonely.

I can remember lying in bed at night after saying all the prayers I was supposed to say, and then praying my own private prayers. I would grab the rolls of fat and squeeze them so hard that tears ran down my cheeks as I begged God to take them away. "Please, take away the cause of my humiliation, the things that make me feel so untouchable and unworthy." I didn't bargain, I just pleaded.

In the morning, hoping against all hope, I would pull up my pajama top in front of the bathroom mirror only to discover it was all still there. In my frustration, I would punch it, pummeling myself relentlessly until I ached.

The room was absolutely still. No shuffling papers or sniffing noses, no nervous coughs or squirming children. I didn't know if they were sitting there wondering if I had gone over the edge, or recalling their own similar pleas to God. At any rate, the words kept flowing.

I don't mean to embarrass you or convince you that I'm strange with this story. But I bring it up because I am willing to bet that it exemplifies more than one of us in this room here today. We lie in our beds in the dark, pleading with God, "Come on, God. I need you now. I can't take it the way it is. Change me so it won't hurt so much, change me so I won't be so alone, or so frustrated, or so frightened. Change something, God. I can't take it anymore."

For a moment a picture of Connie and me in her living room flashed in front of my eyes. Did I really want that to be changed?

We want it to be for real—God's touch, God's blessing. But

they're words we've used so much they've lost their meaning. "God bless you" is what we say when someone sneezes, not when we are bleeding from the soul.

When Jesus keeps saying, "Blessed are the poor in spirit, blessed are those who mourn, blessed are the peacemakers," what comes to my mind is a list of losers. And none of us wants to be in that worst of all categories that we put people into, those we call losers.

Yet, Jesus has a special place in his heart for losers. The hard part is letting go and believing that about him. Perhaps the real power of his words comes through if we put some of them like this:

Blessed are those who are not trying so hard to always be right.

Blessed are those who are not insisting that God do it their way, or that their way is God's way.

Blessed are those who can let go of prejudice and worn out traditions and let God work in new ways.

Blessed are those who can turn from their own desires in order to preserve someone else's love and dignity.

Unexpectedly, a picture of Sandy leaped to my mind, and I stumbled. I tried to cover it with a nervous cough, as I stood there staring at the paper in front of me. Where are these words coming from, I wondered in a panic. What am I saying? Finally, in a hushed voice I got out the last few sentences:

Blessed are those who cry and cry to God but hear no answer.
Blessed are the losers. They know that they need God.
Blessed are the losers. They are the children of God.

TWELVE

"Scott, do you believe what you said?" Sandy asked me as we sat that evening on the patio overlooking the backyard and tree-covered slopes beyond. "About losers, I mean."

"Sure. Didn't it sound like it?" I always feel tired and depressed after preaching, and usually I don't want to talk about the sermon. It makes me feel nervous and edgy, like I've been caught cheating on an exam, or that I've been exposed as a fake.

"Do you think people like Billy or Sonny are losers?"

"I didn't really think about it, to tell you the truth. I just thought about me when I wrote it."

"I never heard you talk about yourself like that before. It's a shame I have to go to church to hear what bothers my husband."

I couldn't tell if she was being sarcastic or genuinely hurt. And I didn't have an explanation for her either way.

"Sandy, I don't do it on purpose," I said, letting out a big sigh. *Why is she like this* I wondered. Why does everything come back to what's wrong with our marriage? It was like being trapped in the Savage River again, with the negatives threatening to overwhelm our life as a couple and drown any remaining love.

"I didn't know your weight bothered you so much. Maybe you could do something about it."

Oh great, here it comes.

"I'd be willing to help you," she added as she reached over and put her hand on my arm.

I cringed inwardly at her touch and sat rigidly, staring straight ahead, silently willing her to take her hand off of me.

"Scott," she said after a while, "am I not enough of a woman for you? I get the feeling lately that you'd rather be with somebody else."

"Like who?" I asked warily, wondering if she had suspicions of her own and, if so, if she had anyone specific in mind? I fought a rising sense of panic as I speculated on where she might be headed with this. This direct approach was not like her. Did she know something she wasn't telling me?

I never found out because the telephone rang.

"It's Esther Savacini," Sandy said, holding the phone out to me as I came in from the patio.

"What does she want?" I asked irritably. The conversation with Sandy had me unsettled and worried, wondering if my mine field of a life was about to explode in my own face.

"I don't know, talk to her." Sandy kept one hand clamped over the mouthpiece as she glared at me. "Go on, Scott, she's your responsibility."

That's when it hit me. I didn't want the responsibility. But I took the phone anyway, acutely aware of the fact that this was all I knew how to do. My life, my training, my hopes and fears, my shortcomings, even my personal life, were all hopelessly bound to the church.

"Yes, Esther, what can I do for you?"

"Reverend Daniels, have you heard? Andrea is home. Isn't that wonderful? I just got home from seeing her, and she's all settled in with nurses there around the clock. Sonny is none too happy, believe me, but Andrea is beaming, absolutely beaming."

I could tell from Esther's voice that she was beaming, too. That was a sight I would have to see to believe.

"No, I hadn't heard," I managed to get in, when Esther paused for breath. "I'm glad for her. She wanted so much to be at home again."

Esther plowed full speed ahead. "She wants to have communion soon, Reverend. I told her you would be glad to come tomorrow."

It didn't come as any great surprise that Esther saw fit to arrange my schedule for me.

"Esther, I don't know if that will be possible. I'll have to check my calendar."

"Nonsense, Reverend. Andrea was thrilled that you came to see her in the nursing home. It's all she talked about. I don't think she's going to disappoint us, trust me. But you need to take that communion to her tomorrow, while she's thinking about it." Esther sounded even happier over this piece of news, although I was totally mystified.

"What do you mean, 'she won't disappoint us?' And while she's thinking about what, Esther? Is there something I should know before I see her again?"

"Now, Reverend, you just never mind. Leave it all to me and I'll take care of everything. Andrea and I are good friends, and I won't let her forget the Westwood Christian Church, you can count on that."

She gave a little laugh that sent shivers down my spine. I had no idea what she meant, but she hung up before I could question her further. Sandy and the kids were in the back of the house, so I headed down to the basement game room. A stationary bike and a fully equipped weight bench gathered dust in the middle of the room. They were supposedly keeping me in shape, but one of us wasn't doing his part. I figured I could take out some frustration and clear my head with a good sweat while trying to decipher Esther's message and Sandy's suspicions. Or were they my suspicions?

I lay down on the bench and wriggled under the bar, wondering when my marriage had left the main road and begun traveling this precarious pathway. Back in seminary I couldn't even begin to imagine myself trying to have an affair with one of the women in my congregation. Yet here I was, wondering if I had time to make a quick call on the basement phone to Connie to see if I could detect any still-smoldering desire in her voice.

"I must think I live in a cheap romance novel," I said to myself as I jerked the bar off the rack and pressed it overhead. Nevertheless, after only two repetitions I replaced the weights and stood up. Instead of going for the phone, however, I stood staring out the window at the moon rising over the mountains.

The sounds from upstairs came from another world—the

bath water running, the giggling and splashing. I felt a pang of regret, thinking of how the nighttime routine usually didn't include me. Next would come story reading, then arranging all the stuffed animals in their proper places on the beds.

Maybe if I was gone, I mused, they wouldn't even miss me. The moonlight filled the sky, casting pale shadows in the backyard. I wonder what it would be like, I asked myself, not to be here anymore, to be on my own. No great shock bowled me over as I tried that on for size. I studied the etchings on the face of the moon, feeling it pull me far, far away.

"Scott?"

I jumped back, ramming my thigh into the weight bar.

"Ow! Don't sneak up on me like that, Sandy."

"I'm sorry. I just wondered what you were doing down here. I didn't mean to scare you." She came over and wrapped her arms around me from behind. I noticed that she had on her oversized pink fuzzy bathrobe.

"Are you going to bed already?"

She ran her hands down the front of my shirt. "If you'll come with me."

I turned around, wondering if I had heard right. She leaned back to switch off the overhead light, then opened her robe and let it drop to the floor.

"I wanted to surprise you. I want you to know that I still desire you and need you."

The moonlight gave her body a luminescent smoothness that took my breath away. I simply stared, mesmerized by her beauty.

"I want you too," I managed to say. Did I need her? I was annoyed with myself for even thinking it. Then that thought was replaced by a sudden urge to tell it all, to let it come rushing out, all the questions, all the fears, the struggle to make sense out of the daily plodding through my life. Maybe even to tell her about Connie.

Instead, as we lay down on her robe, she kissed my eyelids, and her gentleness dissuaded me.

"What's wrong?" she murmured, as I hesitated.

"Nothing. It's nothing. I thought I saw something in the shadows, that's all. Let me kiss it away." And I covered her neck with kisses and softly caressed her hair.

Later, we pulled an old afghan out of a corner and wrapped ourselves in it, giggling at our moonlight escapades. Sandy snuggled under my chin.

"Are you sure everything's okay, Scott? I'll listen to you, you know that."

"I know." I paused, then before I could stop myself, I said, "I'm scared, Sandy. Sometimes I feel so scared and all alone."

She lifted her head from my chest and gazed into my eyes. In the moonlight I saw a tear work its way down her cheek.

"Me too, Scott. Me too."

"Daddy, if all the people disappeared, would God make dinosaurs?"

Sammy peered intently over his bowl of cereal.

The morning dawned bright with sunshine and hope.

"I don't know what you mean, Sammy."

"If all the people in the world disappeared and none were left, do you think God would start all over and make dinosaurs and then maybe whales and stuff, and then people again?" His eyebrows were tightly knit together, and his voice conveyed a sense of five-year-old earnestness.

I fell back on my best all-wise answer. "Uh, Sammy, I don't know." Surely I could do better than that. "What do you think? What would you do if you were God?"

He didn't have to think very long. "I'd make the first people and then I would make Grandma and Grandpa Wertz and Mommy, too."

I pondered that for a moment, wondering why my name didn't appear on the list. Sammy didn't give me long to think about it before he hit me with his next question.

"Daddy, how did God get Grandpa Daniels up to heaven?" Brandy solemnly nodded her agreement to the appropriateness of the question as she downed another spoonful of mushy cereal. "I mean," Sammy continued, "did Grandpa fly? Did you see him go, or is he invisible now? How did he get from earth to God's house?"

"I don't know, Honey. God must know how to get him there since he wanted Grandpa to live with him so badly. Sandy," I called to her back in the baby's room, "our son is turning into a theologian. Quick, talk him out of it."

"Daddy, I'm not a freologian! Do you know what else?"

Oh no.

I mentally ducked. "What?"

"I was God's screwdriver the other day."

I was stumped, while Brandy continued to nod assent, her blond curls bouncing into and out of the milk in her cereal bowl.

"How were you God's screwdriver, Sammy?"

"Well, the day before tomorrow . . . no, that's not right. The day before yesterday—yeah, that's it—Brandy got real sad about Mommy crying. So, I shared my favorite bear with her and didn't hit her once all day."

"Um, uh, I, well that was very nice of you, Son. I'm proud of you. But I still don't know what you mean about being a screwdriver." I also wondered about Mommy's crying.

"Daddy!" They both squealed and shook their heads in consternation over how slow and hopelessly out of touch their father was. They acted like they knew it was their responsibility to lead me around this big world by the hand.

"Don't you remember?" asked Sammy, as he continued in his official spokesman role. "Last Sunday in the children's sermon you brought all the tools you never use. You told us we could be like God's tools if we help our mommies and daddies or other boys and girls. You said we could make good things happen by being the right tool in the right place. So, I was God's screwdriver."

Simple as that. Dummy me, I thought. I got up and kissed each of them on top of the head. "I've got to go to the church, gang. Be good."

"Don't forget it's my birthday soon. Remember, we're

going to go to the Westwood Street Fair and I get to throw the balls at you in the dunkin' booth." Sammy laughed. "Daddy's going to be a big donut and I get to dunk him." They both giggled at the prospect.

"I won't forget. You're going to be six now, so get your arm all limbered up to whip that ball in there."

"It's his fingertips," Sammy said.

"What?" The questions never stop. I wondered how Sandy managed to get a word in. "What's his fingertips?" I asked from the door to the garage.

"God uses his fingertips. When Grandpa died, God used his fingertips to carefully pick him up and take him to heaven."

I stared at him, oddly quieted by his wisdom. Then he pinched Brandy and they ran off to fight it out in front of the television.

Down at the church I decided to head for the bakery and get one of the specialty huge square glazed donuts after I picked up the mail at the post office on the corner. Besides, it was a beautiful morning and I could use the exercise.

Zeke lounged on the steps, a bottle sticking out of the pocket of his grimy coat. His loud snoring startled some scavenging pigeons, who blundered into my way, nearly causing me to stumble and fall.

"Get out of here!" I yelled at them.

"Eh? What did you say? Can't a soul get some sleep?" Zeke sat up, wiping the spittle from his cheek.

"I was yelling at the pigeons, Zeke. Good morning."

"Oh, it's you. I had a visit with you at the church on my social calendar for today." He chuckled and gave me the once over with his good eye. "You're looking pretty chipper this morning."

"Oh, I had a good night's rest, that's all."

"What's her name?" Zeke roared at the lewd implication.

"What did you want to see me about, Zeke?" I ignored his joke, recalling instead the moonlight playing across Sandy's body.

"I wanted to tell you Billy's out of jail."

"That's great. I'm glad to hear it. When did he get out?"

"Last night, I think. Yeah, I think it was then. I remember celebrating at Fat Eddie's." He coughed up a disgusting wad of phlegm and spat it on the sidewalk.

"Is he free, or is he out on bail?" I tried not to look.

"The police questioned the lady some more, said they didn't find any of her stuff on Billy, and since he had only just left her place when they picked him up, there was no reason to hold him." Zeke struggled to his feet and belched loudly. "Something's different though."

"What do you mean, Zeke. Different how?"

"Something's not right with Billy. I saw him at Fat Eddie's, just for a minute, until he saw me and then he left in a hurry. But a father knows when things ain't right with his kid. Maybe it was those cops all pointing their guns at him, or being locked up, but his eyes weren't right. They were kind of far away, dark." Zeke shook his head. "I don't know. Something wasn't right, though."

"I'll try to talk to him again, Zeke. I like Billy. I like talking to him. Maybe I can help."

"Sure, whatever. Hey, Preacher Boy, I hear that snot Sonny Orr accused your wife of stepping out on you up in Cumberland." He spit on the ground again. "The man's an idiot. Don't let it get to you."

"I appreciate the vote of confidence."

Zeke cackled. "Oh, I don't have confidence in nobody, Preacher Boy. I'm not stupid. Sonny is in his own little fantasy world, and he's the only one that doesn't know it. By the way, I hear you preached about being a loser."

I shook my head, bemused. "You sure hear a lot, Zeke."

"Connie told me. She thinks the world of you, you know. She's the best thing that ever happened to Billy and he couldn't see it."

"She's a good woman, that's for sure." I decided to go on to the bakery and come back for the mail. "Well, I gotta go, Zeke."

Zeke fixed his good eye on me and stepped closer, giving me a whiskey breath shower. "Losers are people who throw their lives away without even knowing what they're losing. I know perfectly well what I've lost, Preacher Boy, and the way I see it, that makes me a Christian, not a loser." He leaned back, standing tall, albeit shakily.

"What on earth?" I shook my head, wondering if I'd heard right.

"Yep, the way I figure, your Boss, that'd be Jesus if I'm not mistaken, said that to follow him you had to throw your life away, knowing full well what it is you'd be losing. Well, I've thrown mine away with gusto, and I know exactly what it cost me. My heart, Preacher Boy, it cost me my heart." In a quieter tone he added, "And my son."

With that he walked off down the sidewalk, weaving a bit, struggling to stay erect, but certain, very certain, that he went with God.

THIRTEEN

I decided to take the scenic route from the bakery back to the church so I could enjoy the sunshine a little longer before embarking on the journey to take communion to Andrea Orr. I couldn't resist the sweet aroma from the greasy bag any longer, and I pulled out one of the oversized glazed donuts and took a big bite. Ah-h-h, a gourmet's delight.

I rounded the corner, enjoying my sugar rush, and literally bumped into Esther Savacini coming out of Sonny's video store, sending my donut flying into the gutter and knocking Esther back against a mailbox.

"Yeek!" She squealed. "My gracious, watch where you're going you big . . Oh, excuse me, Reverend, I didn't know it was you."

"I'm so sorry, Esther. Are you hurt? I guess I came around the corner too fast and didn't watch where I was going." I helped her pick up her purse and asked her again if she felt okay.

"I'm fine, Reverend. As a matter of fact, we were just talking about you."

I peered through the storefront, trying to see Sonny past the colorful movie posters that crowded the windows and, with little joy, trying to imagine what the two of them could have been saying. As I mulled that over, Sonny bustled out the front door. As always, he wore a tailored suit with an impeccable tie and perfect hair, as though this little video store contained the corporate headquarters of a Fortune 500 company.

"What happened out here? Can't you two find something better to do than block traffic in front of my store?" He wiped imaginary lint from his lapels, looked around to see if he had an audience besides us, and seeing none, hurried back into the store.

"I'm making my rounds to get donations for the street fair, Reverend. Westwood Christian has to uphold its reputation for raising the most money, you know." Esther leaned closer to me and added, "Every year I get more money out of the merchants than anybody else does, but it doesn't happen all by itself. All people see are the fun and games and the food, but I put in a lot of work nobody knows about. Believe me, it's a struggle, and I'm not getting any younger, mind you. But these young girls in the church don't seem interested in getting involved anymore."

She looked at me with raised eyebrows. "The last minister's wife did a lot in the carnival. She made crafts, sold tickets, organized the helpers, all sorts of things. I didn't see your wife's name on the list of volunteers."

I figured I had better add this to my things-not-to-mention-to-Sandy list. Our marriage had enough pressure on it without the added weight of competing with the last minister's gung-ho carnival queen. I figured my contribution of being the clown in the dunking booth should suffice for both of us.

"No, Esther, what with the baby and all, Sandy's got her hands full. She'll be here to enjoy all the fun though, you can count on that." I hoped that would satisfy her.

"Have you seen Andrea yet?"

"Give me a chance, Esther. I'm on my way today."

"I don't think she has much time, Reverend. The doctors don't give her any hope . . ." She looked away into the distance for a moment. "Sort of makes you wonder, doesn't it? You never know when it will be your turn."

I stayed silent, giving Esther a chance to reveal her own struggles. She dismissed her last thought with a shake of her head.

"But there's always more work to do, right, Reverend? And it's us workers who will see the pearly gates. I'm off to finish my rounds."

I headed back to the church without comment. Down in the kitchen I prepared the home communion set, carefully pouring leftover grape juice into a little bottle and breaking up some slices of bread. I snapped the lid shut and slid the polished box into its velvet bag. In centuries past, people fought and died over the meaning of this simple meal. Grains of wheat crushed, and round, ripe grapes with the life squeezed out of them, combining to give nourishment and energy and something more. I caressed the soft bag.

"I hope it helps you, Andrea, because I sure don't know how to."

I climbed the stairs to the sanctuary holding the communion set and my bakery bag with the other donut still inside. Before going through to my study I sat in the last pew, my chin in my hands, studying the cross in front. I knew Zeke's and Esther's definitions of *Christian* did not match what I had been taught. I smugly noted that I outshone both of them in my dedication and commitment. Then a picture of Sandy in the moonlight flickered across the movie screen in my mind, followed by one of Connie on her living room couch. The one of Connie aroused me more.

"Stop it, you idiot!" I shouted to the empty room. The image of Billy in the jail flashed off and on, until I jumped up and marched down the aisle.

"Well, he's no good for her. What's so terrible about me . . ." I wanted to say "loving her," but the words wouldn't come out. Something more vulgar came to mind.

"I've got better things to be doing," I muttered, and I balled up the donut in the soggy bag and threw it at the cross.

When I arrived at the Orr house, I marveled at its grand appearance. It must be worth a quarter of a million, I figured, with my limited real estate expertise. A circular driveway led through flower beds, with a goldfish pond set in the emerald lawn. I drove up to the flagstone-paved portico.

"Wow," I said aloud, hoping my gawking wouldn't be too noticeable.

As I walked up the front steps and inspected my surroundings more closely, I noticed that the house showed signs of neglect. The shutters needed paint, and one was even hanging by a rusty hinge. The goldfish pond sat empty, the rock gardens on each side of the porch were full of weeds, and the steps were cracked. Apparently Sonny didn't like getting his hands dirty.

I rapped on the tarnished brass knocker. Immediately a ferocious barking came from inside. The oak door shook and trembled, and I hoped it was as strong as it looked. The door knob turned and a scowling woman, huge in her white nurse's uniform, gave me the once over.

"Shut up, Mrs. Beeges. Sit. I said, sit." Her no-nonsense tone had me looking around for a chair so I could obey, just in case she meant me, too.

"Who might you be?" She kept the doorway blocked.

"I'm Reverend Daniels, Mrs. Orr's minister. I brought her communion."

"Come in, Preacher. Wait here in the hallway while I go ask Mrs. Orr."

I eased through the doorway and gingerly closed the door behind me, then pressed myself against it because three feet away sat the biggest German shepherd I had ever seen. It had enough sense to obey the nurse's orders also, and this sentry sat unmoving, head cocked to one side, staring me down.

I slowly turned my head to look around. Gigantic potted plants lined the entrance hall, giving me the uneasy impression that I was trapped in a jungle by a drooling predator. To my left, a dark latticework of wood separated the hall from the living room, which was tastefully decorated with comfortable-looking furniture, pleasant pictures, and other art objects. No wonder Andrea wanted to get back home, I thought. This is what she wants to enjoy each day while she can.

The nurse reappeared at the end of the hall and motioned for me to follow. I warily eyed my guard, hesitant to move. The nurse put her hands on her massive hips and uttered a one-word directive: "Beeges!"

The German shepherd hauled herself erect and backed up a few paces, still eyeing me. Finally the dog turned, bounded down the hall, and disappeared. Only then did I make my own way toward the nurse.

I followed her through a doorway and stopped to gape, openmouthed. Flowers filled the room—on the dressers, the windowsills, a desk, and even the chair. The only unoccupied spot was a bedside potty seat. Andrea lay in a hospital bed covered with bright floral-patterned sheets and several pillows propping her up. When I came in, she smiled and stretched both hands toward me.

"Scott, quite a difference from the last time, isn't it?" Her voice sounded light and happy.

I went to her bedside and took both of her hands in mine. "Yes it is. I'm so glad you're able to be home, Andrea."

"It feels marvelous to be here," she said, throwing back her head and laughing.

I looked around for a place to sit, not relishing the thought of serving communion from the only flower-free seat in the room, the potty chair.

"Take those flowers, Trina, and pull that chair over here by my side for the Reverend." The nurse instantly obeyed, smiling at Andrea but not at me.

When she left, I sat down and said, "I'm not even going to ask how you're feeling. But where did all the flowers come from?"

Andrea laughed again. "Now that I'm home my friends are coming by to visit. They know how I love my gardens around the house and how much I miss working in them. They bring flowers so I can still experience the smell and beauty right here in my little world of a room."

I placed the communion set on the bed while Andrea bubbled on. "It has been such a relief, Scott. Sonny made a stink, of course. He means well, I'm sure. But I've got my own nurses around the clock, and Mother is right here so I can keep an eye on her, the poor dear. She's not always sure exactly where she is, but it helps to be in a place she's familiar with. I hope you can meet her before you go."

"Fine, I'd like to meet her. I've met Mrs. Beeges, but I'm not sure she was too impressed with me."

Andrea giggled. "She's such a worrywart. I think she

believes someone is going to take me away again." Her expression turned serious. "I wish she had been able to keep me out of that horrid place."

"I'm glad you came home."

Andrea gave me a warm smile. "Me too. How do you like this robe Esther brought me?" It was pale yellow with lacy trim. "She's such a dear friend. I don't know what I'd do without her."

After admiring the robe, I said, "I brought communion. Maybe we could do that first before you get tired."

I noticed that despite her brighter attitude and outlook, she was noticeably thinner and her skin had taken on a waxy, yellow hue.

"Yes, thank you, I'd like that very much, Scott." Andrea paused, then continued. "You know, some mornings I wake up in my room and for a few fleeting moments I don't remember. Oddly enough, it's when I look around at all these flowers that I'm reminded of what's happening to me." A wistful tone crept into her voice. "Flowers should remind people of life, not death."

I reached over and took her hand. "I wish I could make it better for you."

"Oh, you do. You help in ways you don't know, Scott. Like bringing me communion today. That means a lot to me."

I busied myself for a few minutes readying the elements. As I began reading the words of the ancient ritual, thunder sounded far off. As it rumbled across the sky, I echoed the cadence of life and death, pain and healing. While we chewed the bread, an explosive crash shook the house, followed by the sound of rain pelting against the roof and the rocks in the garden outside the window.

I made a move to close the window, but Andrea stopped me, saying, "No, please leave them open. I just want to listen."

We sat for a while without speaking, listening to the musical rush of water through the flower beds outside. The leaves of the vines and bushes rustled and swirled as they bowed and curtsied in their dance with the rain.

"I love the smell of rain," Andrea murmured.

As I handed her the communion cup, there was another peal of thunder. Her eyes sparkled, reveling in the chorus of the storm. Communion indeed. I sensed she was savoring a feast, one she would not be denied, even as a benediction on her life.

While putting everything back in the case, I noticed Andrea trying to stifle a yawn. She caught my glance and apologized. "I'm sorry. They have me on the hard stuff now for my pain."

She put her head back on the pillows and stroked her own cheek with her fingertips. "I wish Charles were here to help me. He was so strong, I felt everything would always be fine as long as he was around. I do miss him so. Maybe this would be more bearable with him here."

I sat quietly, watching a faint smile play across her lips. "We literally grew up together, since we were just kids when we married. Believe me, we had some real humdingers for fights. I'd always win, of course, and he would feel so badly about arguing that he would buy me whatever I wanted."

Her hand went to the gold chain around her neck. "He just loved to spoil me. He bought me this chain right before he died. Don't tell Esther, but I'm going to give it to her before I go. I want her to have it, and I'm afraid Sonny will sell everthing instead of doing what I want, so I'm going to give it to her next time she's here."

The storm continued its fierce serenade, and Andrea whispered, "Why is it so hard?"

"I don't know," I found myself whispering in response.

"I've made a lot of mistakes in my life, Scott. I'm going to do what I can to correct some of them in my will. I own a farm out in Garrett County that's been in my mother's family for generations. I loved to go there in the summer and play in the hay, watch the chickens, or wade in the creek beyond the pasture. I have control of it now since Mother isn't able to take care of anything. I've decided to give it to my cousin in Romney. We've never been close, but she's the only other family I have, and I want her to know I was thinking of her. Besides, Sonny would probably sell it, too, for the cash, and this way I'll know it stays in the family."

I hesitated before asking, "How has Sonny been since you came home?"

Thunder rumbled, and I could feel the floor vibrate through the seat of my chair.

"Distant. Sonny is distant. I can tell he resents the nurses being here, and he fusses about the dog and about my mother. Did I tell you, I'm going to leave the house to Mother? She's always going to have a home. No nursing home for her, and I'll leave money specified for her care until she dies."

She stared out the window before continuing. "It's funny, but I never figured my mother would outlive me. I'm glad I'm able to take care of her, though. Sonny will have a fit when he finds out about the changes in the will, but he'll just have to live with it."

Silent tears trickled down her cheeks. "It's all I really have, Scott. Isn't that a miserable epitaph?"

"What do you mean?"

"Money. All I have at the end of my life is money. My mother's mind is gone, my son doesn't care about me, and I don't have Charles to help me through this. All I have left is my money to try and leave some kind of a legacy. The rest of it goes to Sonny, the big crybaby."

She took a tissue from the bedside stand and vigorously wiped her cheeks. "He's never worked for it. It was Charles and I that built up the investments, built this house. Sonny will waste it all in no time, but what else do I have, Scott? He won't take my love. I have to leave it to him so he'll at least know how much I do care for him."

She bent her head and sobbed. "Oh God, why?"

Attila the Nurse poked her head through the door. "Mrs. Orr, it's time for your next pain shot."

"Give me a moment, Trina. Those things make me drowsy, and I want to talk some more with my friend here, the Reverend."

"It's up to you, Honey. You just let me know." Then she turned and gave me a look that would freeze the rain into ice before it hit the ground. I figured it was time to go.

"I'd better go see if my car will start." I gathered my case and prayer book in preparation to leave.

"What's the matter with it?" Andrea didn't seem to want the afternoon to end.

"Oh, it's getting old, I guess. I've been looking at new models, trying to figure out how to afford one. You know how car salesmen are, spouting off all these numbers and specs, talking about overhead cams, drive trains, fuel injectors. I know where to put the gas in and how to turn the key. That's about as far as I go with cars."

Andrea laughed. "Just be sure to pick the right color, that's all I know about cars. I like red ones. Now, Charles was the one who knew about cars. He wanted to buy me one a couple of years ago and started bringing home all sorts of brochures and comparisons in magazines. Salesmen were always calling the house trying to make him a deal. Finally I said, 'Just get me a red one, a big, bright red convertible.' And he did. It's in the garage right now. I loved driving it around town, the top down, wind in my hair. Everybody knew when I was coming down the street."

"Now that would be a sight to see," I chuckled.

"Oh, believe me, it was." She let out a big sigh. "I wonder if there are any red convertibles in heaven. If not, I may ask to come back."

We both laughed. I said my goodbyes and made a mad dash through the downpour. I caught sight of my bedraggled reflection in the mirror and stuck my tongue out at it. Driving along the rain-washed streets I tried to imagine myself telling Sandy about the afternoon, conveying the deep sense of wonder that crept over me while dealing with the realities of life and death and the human spirit, my own questions and fears, my need for the stilling of the storm within, my struggle with thunder and grace in my own soul.

"What's the use?" I muttered. One night of love in the

moonlight didn't magically recreate a sense of devotion and excitement in our marriage, at least not in my eyes.

What did get me excited was thinking about Connie. Surely God didn't want me to be miserable, not when I was trying so hard to be a good servant by preaching, comforting the dying, and putting up with all the hypocrites in the church. Hey, I wasn't the one that wanted to be a minister in the first place. I was tired of paying the price. After all, I'd been doing it all of my life. Something about that line of reasoning rang hollow, but I was getting better at ignoring that empty feeling and pursuing what would make me happier. And what would make me happy would be continuing where I had left off with Connie.

I studiously avoided my own eyes in the rearview mirror. I was not being a hypocrite; I was just trying to get what I was owed. Besides, who could it hurt?

FOURTEEN

"I've forgotten how to pray."

Zeke belched loudly and dug one finger into his ear as he continued. "I mean, I know the words to church prayers still, like the Lord's Prayer, but I can't get myself all worked up into the folded hands, pious routine anymore."

We were seated around the kitchen table. Connie and I sat on one side facing Zeke, who poured another generous measure of scotch into his coffee.

"As far as I'm concerned, a little bit of religion is all most people can handle, or want to handle." His words ran together as he downed his third cup of coffee. "Take that Savacini broad. She's got her own little set-up going in the church, just like Sonny Orr has his little kingdom there, too. I can get that kind of stuff anywhere else, so why would I want to put up with it in the church?"

He wiped his mouth with the back of his hand after draining his cup in one loud gulp. "Now faith, that's something else. Faith is all or nothing, Preacher Boy."

He noisily pushed his chair back, went to the sink, and rinsed out the mug. When he had gone, Connie took my hand in hers and asked me, "Have you seen Billy lately?"

That threw me. I had been sitting there waiting for a signal that she wanted to pick up where we left off, not a reminder that she was somebody else's wife. When I first arrived she greeted me with genuine affection as she showed me into the kitchen where Zeke sat nursing his mug. This was the first mention made of Billy.

"No, I've been busy." It came out defensively, but I didn't know if I was defending how I spent my time or who I spent it with.

"I just wondered," she said as she snuggled against my

shoulder. "He hasn't come here since he got out of jail, and Mikey's been missing him."

"Nope, I haven't seen him."

"Scott, what do you see in me?" She kept her head down so I couldn't see her face. "I mean, you're risking an awful lot by hanging around with me and, you know . . ." She left the thought unfinished, but I knew what she meant. "What do you want, Scott?"

I cleared my throat, stalling for time. It wasn't like I didn't think about it all the time, but I never pictured myself coming up with a straight answer, especially to her face.

"I need you." I kissed the top of her head. "That's all I know. I need you. You are my promise of what could be, of letting go and discovering what it is to be real and not a robot of a human being." I sighed. "That doesn't even make sense, does it?"

She laughed. "No, but it sounded good. That's what I like about you. You make me feel like I am somebody, and you talk to me like I'll understand what's going on in your thoughts."

"If you figure them out, how about letting me know what they mean," I said wistfully.

"I'll tell you a secret, Scott. It excites me. Now isn't that a terrible thing to tell a preacher? But it does. I think, here's this man with all his education, who comes from a whole other world than these hills and hollows, and this man pays attention to me, he knows and understands what it is for me to be lonely."

She turned her face up toward mine. "I know it's wrong, but it makes me want to grab on to you and not let go. It makes me want to give you everything I've got."

Connie put her arms around my neck and crushed her lips against mine. The fierce hunger in her kiss took my breath away. Here it was, what I wanted, what I ached for, somebody wanting me with total, uncontrolled passion. I felt giddy and dizzy.

And scared.

My sense of foreboding grew stronger as our kissing continued. I tried to push it out of my mind, but it wouldn't budge. Connie pressed her body against mine, kissing my neck as I fumbled with the front of her blouse. I silently screamed at the nagging fear to shut up. I wondered who would win the race, my body or my conscience. I didn't know which one I was rooting for as our passion intensified.

"Mommy?"

We both gasped. Mikey stood in the kitchen, trailing a tattered blanket behind him. Connie hurriedly rebuttoned her blouse while I clumsily stood up.

"Mommy's here, Sweetie." She turned Mikey around and led him back to the bedroom. I fled.

As I came out the front door I was still trying to get my shirt tucked into my pants. I looked up and to my horror, a large red convertible slowly cruised past with the unmistakable figure of Sonny Orr in the driver's seat.

"Please don't let him see me," I muttered, as I ran the last few yards to my car and got in. I backed out of the driveway and took a quick look at the front door. Connie stood there, her hand over her mouth. In the dim light I couldn't make out the expression in her eyes, and I had no desire to see my own.

Needless to say, I couldn't get to sleep after I quietly stole into bed at home. Sandy's steady breathing mocked me, and I irrationally started to get angry at her for being so undisturbed. I thought of a hundred reasons why it was her fault that I ended up in Connie's arms. My desperate prayers didn't even reach the ceiling. "Why should they?" I asked myself. "I'm an idiot, an idiot, a real slimy, disgusting idiot."

I squeezed my eyes shut as tight as I could. All I saw was Mikey and his blanket. It reminded me of how I used to get to sleep when I was a boy. I decided to try it, hoping that if I could sleep, the whole mess might go away by morning.

I began to slowly roll my head from side to side on the pillow. It made a soft rustling in my ears as my head went back and forth, back and forth. As a child I used to sing to the hypnotic rhythm, calling for my mother to come chase away the ghosts and shadows. Now in this bleak darkness, as first one ear and then the other brushed against the pillowcase, I could dimly hear the childish chant whispering in my head until I drifted off.

"Mommy, hey Mommy. Mooommmmy, hey Mom-mmy."

The dream returned to haunt my sleep. It began with me in the sanctuary of the church, walking down the center aisle, the huge windows looming on both sides. I walked from the front of the room in the gloom, my eyes fixed on the doorway at the back, trying to penetrate the black hole that lay beyond it. All was quiet, perfectly still. The hairs on the back of my neck stood up as I tried to keep myself from turning around to look back at the pulpit and the cross behind me.

Halfway down the aisle I couldn't bear it any longer, and I took my eyes off the black doorway to peer back over my shoulder. The chancel was empty. No people. No ghosts. Just as my eyes came to rest on the cross, there was a loud snapping sound.

As I watched in terror, the windows on one side swung open, and I felt a rush of warm, stifling air on my face. I tried to run, but my feet refused to obey my brain. Then the mist came through the windows, the same white, swirling mass as before. It danced above the pews, oozed toward the floor, and then suddenly swirled up to the chandeliers. With a blast of icy air the mist seemed to turn its focus on me, surrounding me, tugging at my robe and vestments. Of its own power, the mist began to push me toward the open window.

Resistance was useless. I tried to grab the ends of the pews as they slipped past, but they were wet and slippery, impossible to grasp. The window was drawing closer and closer. I tried to scream, rolling my head from side to side, as a roaring filled my ears.

My whole body began to shake, my arms and legs flapping loosely in the air. A voice came through the open window, echoing dimly from a great distance.

"Da-ad-dy, hey, Da-ad-dy!"

The shaking stopped, then started again. Drops of water struck me on the cheeks and forehead. My hands refused to wipe the drops away.

"Daddy, come on. Wake up!"

I opened my eyes to find blue eyes in giggling faces looking down at me. Sammy and Brandy were in wet towels, fresh from their morning baths. Their soaked hair dripped onto my face as, perched on each side and pinning down my arms, they continued shaking me and trying to roll me off the bed.

"What are you doing?" I asked irritably.

They both froze, eyes wide, their glee instantly turned to fear. Just as quickly my surly mood evaporated. *What was I doing?* In one motion I sat up and captured them in my arms, tickling their bellies. They screamed in delight.

"Who wants ice cream for breakfast?" Without waiting for an answer, I jumped off the bed and ran down the hall. They followed, yelling at the top of their voices.

"What's going on?" inquired Sandy, a smile on her face as she fed the baby. "It's past 8:30. I thought you'd never get up," she teased me.

"Daddy said we could have ice cream for breakfast!" Sammy and Brandy jumped up and down.

Sandy laughed as I came around the counter into full view.

"Ah-ha, I caught you with your pants down!"

I stopped in mid-stride, ready to protest my innocence, feeling the blood rushing to my face. How could she know about last night, I wondered in a panic. She pointed to my legs. With relief I realized I was standing there, surrounded by shrieking children, wearing nothing but my underwear. Sheepishly I backed down the hallway to get some pants.

Later, as we smacked our lips over fudgy marshmallow ice cream, I looked around the table at my family. The kids had chocolate smeared everywhere on their hands and faces. Sandy looked more contented than I had seen her in quite a while.

"I don't know who's crazier, you for wanting ice cream for breakfast or me for going along with it." She shoved a big spoonful into my mouth. "Next you'll be declaring chocolate chips are really vegetables."

The phone rang. I snatched it off the receiver with a theatrical flourish and answered, "Daniels's Ice Cream Emporium."

Over the kids' giggling I heard sputtering on the other end. "What the . . . Who is this?"

That same belligerent, blowhard tone. *Oh, no, not now.*

"This is Reverend Daniels, Sonny." I motioned to the kids to settle down, the hilarity instantly drained from the moment.

"Daniels, I've had it!"

I held the phone away from my ear and gave Sandy a resigned shrug of my shoulders. "What's wrong now, Sonny?"

"Don't patronize me, you creep. This time you've gone too far." Sonny spit the words out like bullets.

"What are you talking about?" I fidgeted uneasily in the chair, and Sandy apparently sensed that it was not a social call as she shooed the children back to their bedrooms to get dressed.

"You and Savacini conspiring against me, that's what. That busybody came over last night and Mother gave her some jewelry. Now, this morning, Mother announces that a lawyer is coming to the house this afternoon so she can make some changes in her will."

"Son . . . Sonny . . ." I tried to break in.

"Shut up, Daniels. I'm talking, and I'm telling you right now, you're in big trouble. I've got friends in this church, and they're shocked at what you're doing."

My jaw ached from being clenched, and the back of my neck throbbed. "I didn't do anything," I managed to mutter through my teeth.

"Don't give me that, Daniels. You did plenty, and I'm giving you fair warning. Stay away from my mother. I'm putting her back in the hospital today, and I had better never find you there, do you hear me?" I could hear his heavy breathing through the wire.

His announcement stunned me. "Sonny, you can't do that. You're mother loves being home. She . . ."

"Shut up, Daniels. It's none of your business. Get that through your head. And another thing, it will be a cold day in July before you will ever do my mother's funeral. Do you hear me? Stay away."

The wind rushed out of my lungs. "Sonny, I'm your mother's friend. She isn't even dead yet, for heaven's sake."

"Forget it," he broke in. "I'm in charge here."

With that, he hung up.

I was shaking with rage. I squeezed the phone as hard as I could, but that wasn't enough. Raising it over my head, I smashed it against the wall with all my strength. Pieces of plastic showered the dining area. I stood there, numbly staring at the wreckage of the earpiece, devastated.

Later that day I sat in the back of the sanctuary, only slightly bemused at how innocuous it looked in the daylight when compared to my dream from the night before. I wanted an angel to appear and tell me what to do, to undo my actions of the last twenty-four hours, to show me how to tell Sandy what I needed and what I feared, and to show me how to love her. And while the angel was at it, give me a crash course on being a pastor to these impossible people.

"That's not too much to ask, is it?" I implored the empty room.

Nothing.

Back in my study I busied myself rearranging the piles of papers on my desk. Every time I thought of Andrea going back into the hospital I got nauseated and pictured myself with my hands around Sonny's neck, watching with great glee his eyes bulging while he struggled for breath.

When I heard a knock at the door I momentarily froze, wondering if my angel had actually come. No such luck. Esther Savacini strode through the doorway and planted herself across from me.

"We did it, Reverend."

I didn't like the sound of that "we."

"What do you mean? Did what?"

"Andrea is changing her will. Now, instead of leaving everything to Sonny, she wants to leave half of it to the church." Esther sat down, a look of satisfaction on her face.

"Esther, what on earth are you talking about?" My stomach flooded with acid. "I haven't been visiting Andrea so she would leave the church some money. I don't care what she does with it. She's dying and she needs to know the church cares about her, especially now."

"Andrea is my best friend, Reverend. We went to school together all the way through high school, swooned over the same boys, lied to our parents about where we were going so we could sneak into Baltimore on the train, joined this church together, raised our boys together. Sonny—I don't know—something happened with Sonny. She's so terribly hurt by him, yet he's all she's got." Esther dabbed at her eyes with an embroidered handkerchief. "All he thinks about is that money," she continued, shaking her head at Sonny's greed. "Reverend, she is so impressed with you and all that you've done for her. I mean, I always hoped she would do it, but I didn't know how much."

"I'm lost, Esther. You didn't know how much what?"

"Andrea is leaving the church a half a million dollars. Can you believe it? Originally Sonny was supposed to get it all, but now he gets half and we get half."

There was that "we" again. "Esther, I swear, I never said anything to her about leaving money to the church. The thought never crossed my mind. I just wanted to help her, that's all." I felt no pleasure in the money, and a part of me wondered why. "Sonny called me this morning and told me he's putting Andrea back in the hospital, Esther. And he told me to stay away from her, even to the point of not allowing me to do her funeral."

Esther gasped and covered her mouth with one hand.

"No, he can't do that! She can't die all alone in there, Reverend. We have to do something."

"I don't know what to do, Esther. Sonny thinks I was only interested in his mother's money and I won't ever convince him that it's not true." I really did care for her. That thought stayed with me, as though I had never considered it before.

"Well, you won't have to worry about that. I'm the executor, and I'll see that things are done the way Andrea wants them. I'll let you know when the will is all drawn up and signed, and then we can tell the church board."

I wished she would stop saying "we." Esther stood up and left, while I still sat there in the chair, wondering what kind of trouble Sonny would stir up now. The more I thought about it, the more frightened I became, until I convinced myself that maybe I had better stay away from the hospital. Why bring more trouble on myself?

I needed some sugar. I got up and headed for the bakery, lost in my troubles, wondering how things could get so out of hand so fast. I came around the corner past the post office, hoping Zeke wouldn't be waiting, when I saw lots of flashing lights and running figures.

Halfway down the block two police cars blocked the street from both ends and an ambulance was just easing its way past one of them into the center of the street. I ran to get a closer look, but a police officer put out his hand to stop me.

"I'm sorry, sir, you'll have to stay back."

I could tell from his uniform that he was a state trooper, not one of the locals. "I'm a minister. I thought there might be something I could do to help."

He looked doubtful.

"Scott? Scott please help me."

I didn't recognize the strained voice at first. Then I saw Connie break away from two paramedics who were trying to restrain her. The officer let me past.

I stepped around the ambulance with leaden feet, dreading what I would see. A tight huddle of paramedics gathered around a form on the ground. Just as I got to them, I heard one saying, "The state police life flight should be here in five minutes. He's pretty bad."

"Oh no," I whispered, forcing myself to get closer.

The sight of the small, pale face against the asphalt was a blow to my gut. Lying there unmoving, eyes closed, with a thin trickle of blood coming out of his ear, was Mikey. The paramedic ever so gently slipped an oxygen mask over the still face.

"Hang on, little guy," he said.

Stunned, I stepped back. I started to hyperventilate and put my hands on my knees, trying to force my breathing to slow down. As I raised my head I caught sight of a radiator grill a few feet beyond the tiny form on the ground. I looked higher and saw a bright red luxury convertible.

A policeman was talking to someone at the rear of the car. The officer put his hand on the man's shoulder, then closed his notebook. As he stepped away, I froze. The man leaning against the fender, face ashen, hands trembling, was Sonny Orr.

FIFTEEN

The helicopter landed at the high school stadium. The paramedics worked over Mikey, continuing their frantic activity as they loaded him into the ambulance for the short trip to the football field.

I watched helplessly with Connie, every once in a while patting her on the arm. When the squad was ready to leave, Connie turned to me before stepping into the back of the ambulance, her voice a frightened whisper.

"Scott, please, would you go find Billy and tell him? Please, I need him and Mikey needs him. We'll meet you at the hospital."

I nodded dumbly, then watched until the flashing lights disappeared around the corner toward the waiting chopper. I began to walk quickly toward the church to get my car. That wasn't fast enough, so I started to jog. Panic surged through me until I was running full speed.

I sped off toward the American Legion bar with tires squealing. The car jerked to a halt in the back parking lot, and I left the motor running as I ran through the door and down the hallway. The lights and smell reminded me momentarily of the night Joey shot himself, which seemed like a hundred years ago now. I searched the room with my eyes, spied Billy at the pool table, and quickly crossed the smoky room.

"Billy!" My frightened panting caused Billy to stop what he was doing.

"We've got to stop meeting like this, Preacher," he began.

"Billy, listen to me. Mikey's been hurt. He was hit by a car. Connie is on the life flight with him. She wants you to come."

Billy's face went white. He threw down the cue, cursing as he frantically searched for his car keys. I ignored the questions thrown at me by the others there and grabbed Billy by the arm, pulling him out to my car.

As we roared off toward Cumberland, Billy started pleading, "Please, God, no. Please, not Mikey. Please, not Mikey."

Driving with one hand, I reached over and gripped his shoulder with my other hand. Billy seized it and hung on tight.

The closer we got to the hospital, however, the more Billy withdrew into himself. He let go of my hand and stared out the window.

"This never would have happened if I wasn't such a terrible dad. I've ended up just like my old man and now I'm paying the price." His voice was barely audible.

"Billy, that's not true. This isn't your fault. It was an accident. Mikey ran out into the street and Sonny couldn't stop."

Billy turned to look at me with tortured eyes. "Sonny? Sonny Orr did this?"

I watched him warily as I answered. "Yeah, Sonny hit him. But it was an accident, really it was."

"Sonny is a hopeless idiot." Billy sagged in the seat, leaning his head against the window while he chewed the ends of his mustache.

When we reached the hospital, Billy burst out the door, running for the emergency entrance before the car came to a stop. I followed behind him, but stopped in my tracks at the sight of Billy and Connie, arms around each other, foreheads on each other's shoulders.

Out of the corner of my eye I saw a green-costumed man approaching from the far end of the trauma unit. I could hear Billy whispering to Connie, "It's okay, Baby. Everything will be all right. I'm here, Honey, I'm here."

As the doctor approached, I stepped closer. Everything seemed to decelerate to slow motion, and all other sounds died away. The doctor's face was grim, the front of his smock brown with blood. His eyes said it all.

"I'm sorry, Mr. and Mrs. Simpson. We did everything

we could, but I'm afraid there was just too much damage. We couldn't save him."

Connie collapsed, sobbing, against Billy. I could see his jaw muscles working furiously as he clenched his teeth, unable to speak. The doctor stood there for a moment, shifting from one foot to the other.

"A nurse will be out soon to talk to you." He turned to leave.

"I want to see my baby. I have to see my baby, Doctor." Connie let go of Billy and started after the doctor.

He put out his arms to fend her off. "The nurse will get him cleaned up and then take you back. Now, please, I have to attend to my patients."

He retreated down the row of curtained cubicles without looking back. Connie stood there watching him go, while Billy rocked back and forth on his heels. Rooted to my own spot, feeling a sense of unreality, I hoped I was seeing a bad play being acted out in front of me. The three of us stayed in our positions for a few minutes as though waiting for someone to give us our next lines.

Finally Billy walked up behind Connie and began rubbing her back while whispering into her ear. He led her over to some chairs, all the while talking softly and gently to her. I sat down nearby, numbed by the suddenness of the tragedy, trying to cope with the image of Mikey standing in the kitchen, trailing his blanket, looking in wide-eyed innocence at his mother and me the night before, contrasting with his broken body on the pavement.

Maybe the doctors are wrong, I wildly speculated. Maybe they made a mistake and it's not really Mikey in there. No, he's back at his grandmother's in Westwood. It's all been a huge error, and all we need to do is call her and straighten out this whole mix-up.

"Preacher?"

Billy broke the spell of my fantasy.

"I'm sorry, Billy, I guess I'm at a loss for words."

"Yeah, well, Connie and I were wondering if you would go in with us to see Mikey?"

His bloodshot eyes were hollow with pain. For a moment it was the same look I saw when he came to me in the river that day on the mountain. I shook my head to clear my mind of the image.

"No? You won't come in?" Billy looked confused.

"Oh, I'm sorry, Billy. Yes, I'll come with you. I was just thinking ... well," I fumbled for words, "I—I just can't believe it. I just saw him yesterday, and now, he's ... he's ... gone."

Billy bowed his head and dug his fists into his eyes, his shoulders sagging in defeat. I pushed my mind off of myself, leaned over, and put a hand on each of them. Their sobs filled the waiting room and echoed down the coldly lit corridors.

"Dear God," I whispered, "give them strength. Give me strength."

A nurse appeared, offering to lead us to Mikey. I tried to steel myself, tried also to think of what I could say to Connie and Billy that might possibly help at such an awful time. My heart beat faster as we approached a cubicle with dimmed lights.

"We've cleaned him up, Mr. and Mrs. Simpson." She spoke in an efficient but not unkind voice. "You can go in now. I'll be nearby if you have any questions."

A thousand questions raced through my brain. I wondered if she could answer the biggest one—why?

"It's okay," Billy was saying to Connie. "He needs to know we're still here with him."

We stepped through the opening in the curtains. Mikey's body looked tiny on the white sheets, so still and quiet. All the lifesaving equipment had been removed and a loosely wrapped hospital gown covered his chest and torso. One side of his head was oddly flattened, but otherwise he looked like he was sleeping peacefully.

"Mommy's here," Connie crooned. "Mommy's here, Sweetie."

She bent over to take him into her arms, gently rocking

and swaying while looking into his face. Billy stood beside her, hand on her shoulder, tears streaming down his cheeks.

"I should have protected him," he said in an urgent tone. "I should have taught him how to read the jungle."

I frowned, puzzling over his words. *What did he mean by "read the jungle"?* I dismissed it as the incoherence of grief. It was a mistake I've always regretted.

Hours later I drove them back to Westwood as evening fell. Connie spent a long time with Mikey's body, until finally the hospital staff insisted we leave. Before departing for home, she and Billy walked down to the old C & O canal and wandered about aimlessly while I watched from a distance. Now they huddled in the back seat, clinging to each other as if afraid to let go. My heart ached for them as I drove, and I shuddered at the disquieting question of whether I could bear it if it were one of my own children.

Back at Connie's house Billy took charge, beginning to make the necessary phone calls, urging Connie to get some rest, thanking me for my help. An eerie, steely calm had settled over him at some point during the ride home.

"Preacher, I'm going to pack a few things for Connie and take her to her mother's. She shouldn't have to stay here where all of Mikey's toys and crayons are lying around where he left them this morning before . . ." He stopped but didn't lose control of himself.

"Billy," I urged him, "you don't have to do all this. Let me get some help here for both of you. I'm sure the ladies at the church would be glad . . ."

He cut me off emphatically. "No. Mikey is my son, and I will be here for him. Nobody is going to get him ever again, I'll see to that."

"Okay, Billy." I awkwardly shifted from one foot to the other. What could I do? There had to be something. I hated feeling so useless.

"I'm going to go check on Connie, Preacher. You know the way out."

He went back to find her, leaving me alone in the living

room. For some reason I wandered into the kitchen and stopped dead in my tracks. I stared at the two coffee mugs still sitting on the table where Connie and I had left them less than twenty-four hours earlier. The memory of my desire mocked me and filled me with self-loathing. What kind of a hideous monster was I turning into?

I ran away into the night.

I got into my car and started driving, down the mountain, away from home, away from Westwood, determined to escape my own hell. I took the curves too fast and drove through the red light at the main intersection. The car rattled over the bridge above the Potomac, and I turned toward the mill. Once past it, I would climb Backbone Mountain and then head into the unknown.

The paper mill belched smoke and steam. It ran twenty-four hours a day, seven days a week, turning out glossy paper for slick magazines. Its tanks and towers dominated the skyline and the lives of all those around the sprawling complex. Family schedules competed with production schedules, but there was really no contest. The constant smell of sulfur from cooking pulp invariably brought the same response from locals to those who complained of the horrible stink: "It smells like money to me."

A lumbering pulpwood truck forced me to go at a snail's pace past the eerie orange lights and dull rumblings of the mill. I idly watched the activity of boxcars being loaded with pallets of paper, and then I glanced up as I went under the trestle. Out of the corner of my eye I spotted a lone figure balancing on the end near the hillside above the river. I instinctively knew it was Zeke.

Without thinking I pulled over to the berm and got out. I scrambled up the hillside and found Zeke sitting on the rails, clutching a brown bag with a bottle inside.

"Zeke, what are you doing up here?" My own escape temporarily on hold, I remembered Connie telling me about Zeke's fall from this trestle.

"Aww, Preacher Boy, we both know it should have been me and not poor Mikey."

He tipped the bag to his lips and took a long drink. "You want some?" He offered me the bottle.

"No, thanks, Zeke. Mind if I sit down?"

"What do you see when you look at me, Preacher Boy?" he asked, motioning to the cold steel rail beside him.

I sat down, warily. His question sounded too much like Connie's from last night, and I didn't want to be reminded at the moment of my deceitfulness.

"I, uh, I—I see, well, I see a man." I ran out of words and thoughts.

"You see a disgusting waste of oxygen and human spirit, now admit it. Come on, you can say it. Nobody from seminary is here to tell you to lay off or to make sure that you say that I'm a poor lost soul who needs understanding and generous support to live up to my God-given potential and all that other baloney. I'm a sad, old, disgusting drunk. Be honest for once in your life, Preacher Boy."

I studied the ground, avoiding his eyes.

"Come on, show some guts, I tell you!" Zeke grabbed my arm and pulled me toward him, forcing me to look. "What do you see? What am I? Half animal, half human? That would be generous in some people's eyes." His good eye blazed in the hellish glow from the mill below, and his bad eye stared blankly from the shadows.

I shook my arm free, wanting to slap him as hard as I could. Why had I bothered to stop? Zeke was obviously smashed out of his mind.

"I wanted to tell you I'm sorry about Mikey." I stood up to leave.

"Oh no you don't. You're not getting off that easy, Preacher Boy."

Zeke gabbed my arm again, stood up, and started pulling me farther out onto the trestle. The ground fell away steeply beneath the ties and looking down made me dizzy. I resisted, screaming at him to let me go, but his grip was too strong. He nimbly stepped from tie to tie, forcing me to do the same or go plunging over the side. Fifty feet out over the river he stopped and sat down.

My chest heaving, my legs shaking, I wasn't about to try the trip back on my own. I gingerly sat down next to him.

"What if a train comes?"

"What if one doesn't, Preacher Boy? Then we'll both have to either jump or go back and put Mikey in the ground."

We sat for a moment in silence.

"What were you doing up here?" I asked.

"Waiting for somebody to tell me what I am."

He stared out across the water, tilting his head as if listening to the wind.

"What are you doing up here?" he asked, without turning to face me.

I studied his profile, wondering what he had been like before he turned into . . . this.

"I'm waiting for somebody to tell me what I am, too, I guess. I just didn't know it at the time."

"It hurts, Preacher Boy." He looked beyond the nearly invisible horizon formed by the deep black of the hills and mountains against the star-speckled night sky. "Mikey was a good boy. You know, I never looked at him and said, 'That's my grandson.' I just thought, there is a good boy. Maybe I didn't want to contaminate him with being in my bloodline. It just ain't fair for him to die."

"Yeah."

After pitching the bottle down into the depths below, Zeke fixed both eyes on me and asked, "Do you believe in the suffering of the innocent—that innocent people pay for the sins of the rest of us?"

I shrugged my shoulders. "Even if you believe it, you don't want it to be true, and yet you feel guilty for believing it and hoping that it is true. Otherwise, the rest of us might not get the opportunity to find our way home to God."

Zeke studied me for a long moment, his crooked mouth

partially open and his alcohol breath making me wonder which of us was crazier for being out here.

"You know what your problem is, Preacher Boy? You're careless about what you're becoming. Pay attention to it."

With that he stood up and started back, leaving me stranded.

"Hey!" I shouted after him. "How do I get back?"

"Crawl," he yelled back over his shoulder. "If you can't stand up and walk, then crawl. You'll make it. Don't take too long, though. There's a train coming in two minutes."

Back in my car, I turned around and headed for home. I couldn't figure out why my run-ins with Zeke always left me so oddly disturbed. Fifteen minutes ago my only thought was to get away, but now I drove back down the main street and headed up Horse Rock Mountain toward home.

Zeke was right. I was careless about what I was becoming, to the point where I was willing to run away and desert my family and career. Maybe there was hope if I started crawling back along the way I'd come.

One thing I knew for certain. I desperately needed to tell Sandy about my life spinning out of control, about losing my bearings and looking for comfort and care in the wrong places. She used to be my best friend. She had been there through it all, ever since we were giggling teenagers in the church lounge, helping, hoping, believing in me. I needed to confess and to get back on track, starting with her. I longed to sit down with her and clear the air, to tell her that I loved her and that I wanted to start over. I didn't consider the pain it might inflict on her. I only knew that I would feel better being honest about the state I was in, telling her by my own choice about being tempted to violate her trust, and winning back her friendship.

SIXTEEN

I pulled into the driveway and got out to open the garage door. The beam from the headlights fell on Billy's paintings, and the gaze from the doe's eyes filled me with a great weariness. Something had to change; I didn't know if I had the courage to admit that it was me.

After I pulled the car in, I shut off the engine and went out to the patio to pray. I sat down on the glider and tried to clear my mind. I wanted to say that I was sorry; sorry for being a failure, sorry for not knowing how to lead people, sorry for wanting to use Connie's loneliness to bolster my own ego, sorry for not living up to my father's standards, sorry for hurting Sandy with broken trust. I wanted to confess it all, no holds barred, and find forgiveness and peace of mind.

But nothing came. Crickets chirped, the woods rustled with night sounds, and the breeze ruffled my hair. But no prayer broke free from my heart. Discouraged, I went into the house.

Sandy had her head down on the kitchen table, and her deep breathing told me that she was asleep. I tiptoed past her and went to the kids' rooms. I spent a few minutes watching each one of them sleep, filled with an overwhelming sense of wonder at the thin line between life and death, between trust and fear. I tried to imagine my father looking in on me in the same way, questioning his own purpose and commitment. The tears that filled my eyes surprised me.

Back in the kitchen I spied a sheet of paper under Sandy's folded arms. Curious, I slipped it from under her and started to read. As I did, I felt the floor dropping away beneath me with a sickening rush. It was a letter, unsigned, addressed to "My dear Mrs. Daniels." It got right to the point.

I thought you might be interested in knowing that your husband is having an illicit sexual affair with a member of his congregation, Mrs. Billy Simpson. While pretending to be a loyal husband and servant of God, he is actually seducing this woman and using her for his own vile and evil purposes. He was seen coming out of her house several times late at night, pulling up his pants and buttoning his shirt. While I do not mean to hurt you, Mrs. Daniels, I think you should know what kind of a man your husband really is—a perverted, unfaithful, money-hungry adulterer.

Signed,

A Friend

P.S. I am also sending this letter to the church elders so they can do what is necessary.

A wave of rage engulfed me, followed by panic. I pictured Sandy reading this note, alone at the table, and I cursed myself for being so gutless. I wished I knew how to grow up.

She stirred and opened her eyes. I tried to read her expression, fearful of an explosion of hate, but her first words were about Mikey.

"I heard about poor little Mikey."

"How did you know?"

"Esther called and told me what happened, that he died on the way to the hospital." Her even tone made me wary.

"Oh, I should have known Esther would be on top of things."

I held my breath, childishly hoping that maybe she would have forgotten about the letter.

Sandy looked at me with concern. "How did it go for you, being at the hospital with Connie? Did you have to tell Billy? Do they know when the funeral is yet?"

I put up my hands to stop her. "Whoa, slow down, Sandy." I sat down across from her, quietly sliding the letter under one leg.

"I'm sorry. I've been worried about you all day," she said. "Did you have anything to eat today? Here I am rattling on with questions, and you're probably exhausted and starving."

"Food hasn't been much of a priority."

I heard the paper crinkle under my leg, reminding me of my interrupted attempt to flee earlier in the evening. Turning back felt more heroic before I discovered the letter. Now she knew that she should not trust me and that I was a liar. I had turned back without any real plan, just the idea that I needed to sort things out and find the time and the way to reconnect with Sandy. The letter changed everything.

"Scott, did you hear me?"

I rubbed my eyes, while trying to figure out what my next move should be. "No, like I said, it's been a long, awful day. What did you say, Sandy?"

"I said, do you want to go right to bed?"

I shook my head. "I'm not sure what I need or what I want."

"Scott, are you okay?" She came around the table and rubbed my shoulders. "Do you want to tell me about the day?"

I sighed. "Seeing that little boy lying there on the street, it felt like something broke inside of me. I drove Billy up to the hospital and I tried to comfort him, to let him know I cared about him and Mikey. But I don't think I did any good. I wasn't anything more than a warm body there with him and Connie. And I kept thinking about how that could be Sammy there. That fragile body all cold and blue could be my son." I stopped to blow my nose.

Sandy kissed me on the top of my head. "Isn't that the kind of person you would want to be with you if it really was Sammy? I know I would. Maybe how you felt about doing it or what you felt while trying to help isn't as important as doing it."

"It's weird," I said, "but Billy seemed to take it better than anyone else. He comforted Connie, and he started making arrangements for everything, all in a calm, rational manner. Yet I know he had to be torn up inside."

"Maybe that's his way of handling it, Scott."

"I guess so, but I still wonder if he's going to be all right."

Sandy laughed. "You worry about him more than you worry about me."

I bristled at that remark. "That's just great, Sandy. Thanks for being so helpful," I said sarcastically.

She sounded annoyed as she said, "I was just kidding, Scott. I know you have to give a lot to others in this kind of work, and I'm really trying to handle that and be supportive. That doesn't mean I always like it, but I do try to understand it."

A wistful note crept into her voice as she continued, "I remember what it was like to have you all to myself when we were first married, how I felt so special and proud to be with you. I still feel that way, Scott, even though I'm not too good at showing it."

Assaulted by my own guilt as I listened to her confirm her love for me, I mentally wrestled with the truth. Reluctantly, I pulled the letter out from under my leg. "Even when you get a letter like this?"

Sandy laughed again, catching me by surprise. "I wondered what happened to that. Can you believe the nerve of some people? What could they possibly gain by making up something like that about you and trying to get trouble started between us? I think it's funny that somebody is accusing my macho husband," she leaned over and patted my belly, "of being such a ladies' man." She added derisively, "And then doesn't have the guts to sign it."

I was dumbfounded. She didn't believe what was in the letter! All I had to do was deny it, and the way would be clear to . . . to what? I shut my eyes, hoping for some flash of inspiration, some guidance out of the blue. The silence stretched out to a minute.

"Scott? Scott, why aren't you saying anything?" Sandy's voice dropped down lower.

I couldn't open my eyes as I heard the fear catch in her

throat. "Scott, this is a joke, right? I just told you how much you mean to me, and you're being silly now, aren't you?"

There was a bad taste in my mouth. After an eternity I opened my eyes and saw Sandy doubled over like she had been struck, gasping for air.

"Scott, please say something."

Her words hung there in a terrible void. I stood up, clinging to the table for support, my precious image of myself shattered forever.

"I—I—I wanted to tell you about it," I began.

"So, it *is* true." She said the words slowly, as if unable to let go of her disbelief.

"I didn't want to hurt you, Honey."

"Don't call me that." Suddenly, her voice was hard, cold. "Don't you dare call me that right after you tell me you're having an affair."

"I didn't want to hurt you. We never really did anything. I just needed somebody to . . ." I shrugged helplessly. "I just needed somebody."

Sandy sounded close to hysteria. "Never did anything? You don't pull up your pants on the way out from doing nothing, Scott." She began walking around the room, pulling on her hair with both hands. "I don't believe this. I don't believe this," she said over and over.

She went over to the door leading out to the patio and leaned her forehead against the glass. "I remember thinking a few days ago that we were turning some kind of corner. Things have been tough, but I felt like I was coming out of it, that I had survived, and maybe now we could get back on solid ground. And now . . . now, you tell me." She suddenly stopped and slapped her forehead, then spun around and glared at me. "That night, Scott, that night we made love in the moonlight. Did you think about her while you were touching me? Tell me, Scott. I want to know."

The rage in her voice made my blood run cold.

"Sandy, stop it. This is hard enough without . . ."

She interrupted with a shriek. "Don't tell me to stop it,

Scott! I'll stop it when I'm good and ready, you worthless excuse for a husband."

Her words stung like a slap to my face. I wanted to sob my heart out, begging for forgiveness, and at the same time I wanted to hit her to make her stop. Didn't she know I had been about to come clean on my own? Didn't she care that I was scared too?

"How could you, Scott?"

The pain in her voice formed a suffocating band around my chest, drawing tighter and tighter. She sat down in a chair and hugged her knees to her chest, rocking back and forth and moaning like a beaten child. I started toward her, drowning in despair, wanting to touch her, foolishly thinking we could comfort each other.

"Don't touch me!" she spat out. "Don't you dare touch me."

I recoiled, helpless. "I don't know why I'm like this, Sandy. I don't know why I can't make myself be everything I want to be. I try, but it always goes wrong. I didn't want to hurt you, Hon . . . Sandy . . . I'm sorry."

Without another word she stood up and rushed past me. I heard her turn the lock on the bedroom door, shutting me out, leaving me alone. My dream of crawling back had turned into a nightmare.

I spent the night listening to Gordon Lightfoot tapes through the headphones. I didn't even try to go back to the bedroom. At times I cried, alternately disgusted at myself, bewildered, and scared about what might happen next. I didn't have to worry about the dream disturbing me because I never slept.

At dawn Sandy came out, her eyes red and underlined with dark shadows that added to the bleakness. We avoided looking at each other as we circled like two weary heavyweight fighters in the fifteenth round.

"Scott, I made a decision." The anguish in her voice tempered my relief at knowing she would still talk to me.

I cleared my throat. "What kind of decision?"

"After Mikey's funeral I'm taking the kids and going to my parents' place in Pittsburgh."

Like a dummy I thought the pain couldn't get any worse. But her announcement sent me to new depths.

Before I could respond, Sammy and Brandy came into the kitchen looking for breakfast.

"Mommy, we want waffles, okay?" Sammy plopped down at the table, while Brandy climbed into my lap.

"Daddy, you smell funny," she said, holding her nose.

I found I couldn't stop looking at the two of them, and I soaked up their banter while they enjoyed their waffles, finding that their presence created a tiny quiet spot in my battered soul. I noticed that Sandy, too, kept looking at them.

When Sandy went to get the baby, out of the blue Sammy asked, "Daddy, tell me about when I was born."

"Me too," chimed in Brandy.

It was a frequent request. They each treated the story of their birth as though it was their personal possession, and the repetition of it became a ritual not to be tampered with or done incorrectly. I didn't particularly feel like telling them, however.

"Not today, gang. Daddy had a long night."

"Come on, tell us. We want to know. It's important, Daddy."

I relented. Maybe it would get me through the morning.

"Okay, well, let me see. Sammy was born one dark night in a strawberry patch where a rabbit family adopted him."

"Daddy," they both shrieked, "tell it right."

"Uh, well, Sammy, you were born when Mommy and I lived in Pittsburgh and Daddy was going to school to become a minister."

"Did you have a houth?" Sammy asked around a gooey mouthful of waffle and syrup.

"No, we lived in an apartment."

"Do I remember it?"

'No, you were too busy making sure that you got enough

bottles and dry diapers and waking me up at two in the morning screaming like a banshee."

I could picture it clearly—recalling the uncertainty mixed with pride as the arrival of The Baby drew near. During the first pregnancy I had been attentive and considerate, watching out for Sandy and worrying and fussing over her all the time. There had been the wonder of hearing the heartbeat for the first time and watching Sandy's belly growing larger every day.

During the second pregnancy I had been less patient and forbearing. Sandy was queasy and worn out most of the time. Two-year-old Sammy was in the middle of potty training and enjoyed his newfound power of resistance. I remembered it as a long, long nine months. Most evenings I found myself alone in the living room by early evening, brooding over the hassle of it all. Still, all in all, both births reaffirmed my faith and deepened my awe. The stories were worth repeating.

"Daddy, what's next? Come on, pay attention," Sammy chided me.

"Sorry, where was I?"

"You and Mommy lived in an apartment in February." Sammy turned to Brandy, who sat enthralled, as if hearing it for the first time. "That's what month my birthday comes. You're in October."

With that clarification, I continued. "Mommy was having a little bit of trouble with her blood pressure getting too high. Probably because you were in such a hurry to get out of there and see what you were missing."

They both giggled. "Doctor Sarah," I explained, "said to come in for an appointment and to be ready to go to the hospital."

Sammy turned again to Brandy to interpret. "Doctor Sarah was the nice lady doctor who delivered me. But not you." Brandy looked hurt. "That's okay, Brandy," big brother then consoled, "you had a different doctor, a man. He did okay."

"Excuse me, can I continue?" I asked with mock impatience. At this rate the storytelling would take all day. But I had to admit the stories were more than entertainment. They were a part of my own story, a vital part. Perhaps even a redemptive element.

"As I was saying, sure enough, when Dr. Sarah checked, Mommy's pressure was too high, so she put her in the hospital."

"Did she explode?" wondered Sammy.

"No, she didn't explode. A couple of days later they gave Mommy some medicine to make her start having the baby. I got all dressed up in doctor clothes and went into the delivery room to be with Mommy."

"Did it hurt to push me out?"

"Mommy said it did. Personally, I didn't feel a thing."

"Daddy, I meant for Mommy."

"Yes, it hurt. But it was also very exciting. We were both eager to meet our new baby, see him, touch him, tickle him, and love him." I wondered if a rebirth would be even more painful.

"Mommy pushed real hard and I popped right out."

"Something like that. Your head came out, and Dr. Sarah told Mommy to stop pushing."

Sammy jumped in, proud to remember. "Because of my billy cord, right, Daddy?"

"That's right. Your umbilical cord had gotten wrapped around your neck three times. Dr. Sarah calmly cut it and unwrapped it, then let you come out the rest of the way. She plopped you on Mommy's tummy and we both said hi to you."

"Did I say hi back to you and Mommy?"

"No, silly. Another doctor took you and started working on taking fluid out of your lungs." I paused, remembering the doctors telling us that our new son had to go to the intensive care unit but not to worry. Not to worry? Yeah, right!

I could still feel the sense of helplessness and overwhelming fear that mixed with the joy and the adrenaline aftershock. While Sandy was pregnant it had all seemed unreal somehow, as I fretted about what kind of a father I would be. All my focus had been on me. The shock of the problems at the birth had thrust me, ready or not, into the real work of being a father—worrying, fretting, comforting, trying to appear calm so Sandy wouldn't get upset, wanting desperately to make everything all right, safe and secure for my son. I learned that I couldn't do that, no matter how hard I might desire it.

"It was snowing when you took me home, right?"

"That's right. You were only in the hospital a couple of days, and we got to take you home in a snowstorm and then we started being a mommy and daddy."

"Was I still all blue?"

I shook my head. I had forgotten to include the part about Sammy coming out all slimy and solid blue. I would never forget that color.

Just like I would never forget the gray, ashen hue of my father's face as they disconnected the breathing apparatus.

"Now me, Daddy." Brandy had waited long enough.

"Yeah, now Brandy, and how Mommy's labor stopped after she started having the baby at church." Sammy, the typical big brother, butted in on Brandy's territory.

She didn't let him get any further. "Sammy, stop it. Daddy, tell him to shut up. You tell the story."

"All right, that's enough. Sammy, be quiet. Brandy listened to your story, now it's your turn to listen."

"Grandma and Grandpa Wertz were there when I was born," began Brandy.

"That's right. They came to stay and help me watch Sammy while Mommy got ready to have you."

"That's because Sammy is so bad." She stuck out her tongue at her brother.

"Brandy, shut up!" he retaliated in a screeching whine.

"Now settle down, both of you." Story time could only last for so long. "We had an old green station wagon. After church one Sunday—"

"In October," chimed in Brandy.

"Yes, in October after church Mommy said it was time. So Sammy stayed with Grandma and Grandpa while we drove to the hospital. On the way the car started to act up, making weird noises and bucking like a wild horse. It scared Mommy so much that her labor stopped by the time we got to the hospital. But after a while it started again and out came Brandy."

"Did I cry a lot?" Brandy already knew the answer.

"You only cried when the doctor or nurses fussed with you. You wanted to be left alone to greet the world on your own terms, snug in your blanket."

"And then you carried me down to the nursery," said Brandy with pride.

"Yep. I picked up the bundle of blankets and carried this little, pink, squirmy creature to the nursery. I rocked you in the rocking chair while the nurses got your bed ready."

Satisfied that they had heard the proper versions of their beginnings, they both hopped out of their chairs and raced to the living room. Sandy came into the room holding the baby.

"I heard the stories," she said softly. "They love to hear them, don't they?" She shook her head in wonder.

"Yeah, they sure do." The stories had been a brief respite from the realities of our current crisis. Now those painful truths rudely intruded once again as we both grew silent, awkward without the children as a buffer.

"They'll be excited about the trip to Pittsburgh," I finally offered.

"Yeah, it will be a big deal." She paced around the kitchen as I searched for some hint of forgiveness in every motion that she made, too afraid to ask.

"Scott, I hate you right now. I wish I could say that it will go away, but I can't. I hate you. I have to go away so I can figure out what to do."

She started to cry, and I ached to go over and hold her, but I didn't think I could stand to see her revulsion for me one more time. So I sat, wishing for a story that would explain it all to me, too.

SEVENTEEN

What would my dad do in this situation? I had to laugh at that thought from out of nowhere. I sat in my office at the church, staring at the phone. Esther had called to tell me that Andrea Orr was failing fast in the hospital, with her major organs beginning to shut down.

"And, oh yes, by the way," Esther said casually, "I thought you might be interested in knowing that a special meeting of the board of elders has been called for tonight to discuss a most grievous situation." It could only be the letter, I was sure of that much.

Right now I needed to be writing a funeral for Mikey. "Take your pick, Dad," I sarcastically hurled at the fuzzy image of him in my mind. "I have been fooling around with another woman; my wife is leaving me; the elders are probably plotting to get rid of me; I'm to conduct a funeral for a little boy killed accidentally by a despicable little man who holds all the cards; there is a woman dying in the hospital because her idiot of a son wants to be sure he gets all of her money and not 'just' half a million; my prayers are returning to me marked 'forwarding order expired'; or, Dad, how about just the general sense of disappointment and disgust with myself that is threatening to send me to the crazy farm. Am I a great son, or what!"

I waited, listening. There were no creaks or groans in the empty building, nothing to tell me what to do or what to say. Esther also told me that she had spoken with Connie. I felt a little pang of jealousy at that bit of information. I still harbored the fantasy of comforting Connie, being the one to hold her, to tell her that I would take care of everything, even bring Mikey back to her. Connie told Esther that she wanted the church and the town to proceed with the street festival. The festival raised money for the day care and nursery school in town, and Connie said that Mikey would have wanted everybody to go ahead with it and have a good time.

So the festival would go on, and I would still have to dress up in the old gay nineties swimming suit and make a fool out of myself in the dunking booth. Esther commented on how brave Connie was, how caring to still insist on the festival going forward in true Westwood spirit.

I gave up on waiting for the funeral muse to inspire me and decided instead to walk over to Mitchell's Mortuary and Fine Funeral Home. How could I keep functioning through all of this turmoil within, I wondered. Yet I kept performing all of my regular duties, going through the motions with people, looking peaceful and in control on the outside while on the inside I was in abject despair. Maybe it would have been better if I hadn't stopped to talk to Zeke on the train trestle but instead kept going out of town, over the mountain, and away into the sunset, never to be seen or heard of again in these parts. It couldn't be any worse than facing the music here.

Arriving at Mitchell's, I went in the front entrance and looked for somebody to show me to the viewing room. The dimly lit rooms and hallways were deserted. I could hear voices upstairs in the office, and I strained my ears to hear if it was Connie or Billy up there making final arrangements. The funeral would be tomorrow morning, followed by a fellowship luncheon at the church, leaving me little time to prepare.

I wandered into what I thought to be a deserted room. At one end, almost completely covered by a mountain of flowers, a silver casket sat with its lid open. I approached cautiously, spooked by my own insecurity, getting the creeps the way I used to as a child when I had to go down into the basement alone. I would always peek over my shoulder, trying to see into dark corners, wondering what could be hiding behind the furnace, dashing up the stairs to safety, two at a time, sure that some nameless dread followed close behind.

Gazing at Mikey's peacefully composed face, I suddenly

felt that same dread, and I could swear the floor was tilting wildly, trying to throw me off balance and onto the cool steel box. I reached out and grasped the edge to steady myself.

The size of the casket struck me as terribly disproportionate. Mikey's child-sized body barely took half the space, making him appear even smaller, lost in the billowy, satin space. I wanted to reach out and shake the tiny figure, tell him to wake up, yell at him that he was worrying his mother to death. *Wake up! It isn't right for you to be lying there looking so calm while the rest of us struggle with chaos.*

And hey, wake up, Mikey! You have to hear that your father loves you. He wants more than anything for you to have a better life than he does, so don't blow it like this. Your daddy is an artist, but he's trapped in this place and his past is killing him, so don't you do this, you hear me? You have no right.

"Get a grip, Scott," I muttered.

"Preacher."

I stared at the pasty face, my heart pounding. I could have sworn I heard my name, or at least what passed for my name around here. I really am losing it, or, I thought irrationally, my wish is coming true. He really isn't dead.

"Preacher, over here. It's me."

The voice sounded familiar, but I couldn't place it. I turned around, mentally chiding myself for such foolish believing. In the doorway sat a skinny boy in a wheelchair.

"I saw you come in here, so I followed you. I wanted to pay my respects, too."

I took a step closer, still puzzled.

"It's me, Joey McCrady." He pushed his stringy hair away from his face and smiled.

"Joey?" It was a ghost after all.

His expression turned somber. "Billy's always treated me like a man, so when I heard about Mikey, I just had to come."

"I don't think Billy is here right now." I studied the apparition in front of me. I hadn't seen Joey since that night in the American Legion hall. "How did you get here?"

I thought I had asked the question only in my mind, but Joey smiled triumphantly.

"I've got my own van now. My parents got some money from the state to get me my own wheels with special controls, a chair lift, the whole bit. It even has a CD player. Cool, huh? The babes really go for it."

I opened my mouth, then closed it. What could I say?

"Anyway, Preacher, I wanted to talk to you. I want to apologize for pointing my gun at you that night. I had too much to drink and I got pretty out of line. I hope I didn't scare you too much."

"Uh, no, no, that's all right, Joey. How are you doing?" Could this get any stranger?

"I'm doing okay, Preacher. My leg is fine and I'm getting ready to go to a rehab training program next month."

"That sounds great, Joey. Your parents must be relieved that they were able to find you one of those schools. I hear they can be tough to get into since there are so few openings."

I wanted to ask him about the contrast of this news with what I remembered of his dad dropping him off at a bar every night to waste time, but his proud expression stopped me. Could he have changed since shooting himself?

"Oh, it ain't my mom and dad that got me in. I'm going to study gun repairs and open my own shop, Preacher." He scratched his head and then wiped his hand on his shirt. "It was old man Simpson."

I furrowed my brow. "You mean Zeke? What did Zeke do?"

"It was the craziest thing, Preacher. I went to Fat Eddie's one night, and Zeke was there shootin' the bull and drinking his whiskey. Out of the blue he asks me what I'm going to become."

"Yeah, that seems to be his favorite question," I said under my breath.

"What's that, Preacher? Did you say something?"

"No, I was just thinking out loud."

"Well, I asks him, what does he mean? Does he mean

what am I going to be when I grow up, which gave me a big hoot, because I'm going to be a cripple when I grow up. Or does he mean what's going to become of me, like when my momma and daddy are gone? And I yukked it up over that one, too, because I can count on the rest of my family and this town to cover for me anytime."

He spread his arms out to his side and searched my face. "But you know what, Preacher? He didn't mean either of those. I mean, I couldn't get his question out of my mind all night. Until it dawns on me, what am I turning into? You know what I mean? I'm going to sit in this wheelchair forever, maybe, but I don't have to act like a crippled idiot forever."

I stared at him, trying to sort out what he had said, and trying to get beyond the image of him waving that big pistol at my face. He appeared to be embarrassed by my intense scrutiny, putting his head down and wheeling his chair over to the casket.

"I'm not real good with words, Preacher, not like you are. I just know it's something I feel in here," and he thumped himself on the chest.

"I'm glad to hear it, Joey." I found my voice, still not sure I knew exactly what he meant.

For a while he looked at Mikey's body, awkwardly crossed himself, and then reached up over the edge of the casket to touch Mikey's hand.

"I don't know if you guys do that stuff with your hands and making the cross, but I want to be sure Mikey gets to the right place."

"I don't think it will hurt, Joey. Who knows, it might help. I'm sure Billy will be glad to know you came."

He turned around and wheeled back to where I stood. After fishing around in his pants pockets, he withdrew a wad of dollar bills from one of them and thrust them toward me.

"Here, this is for Billy and Connie. Promise me you won't tell them it's from me, but I want to give them something to help out. I know times are hard and it costs a lot to bury somebody. I get Social Security disability, so I got my own money and I can do what I want with it. Okay?"

"Okay." I accepted the money, feeling disquieted anew by the transformation before me.

Joey headed for the door. "Oh yeah, I almost forgot, Preacher. Thanks!" he yelled over his shoulder.

"Thanks for what?" I yelled back as he kept going down the hallway.

"For coming that night. The cops would have come in with their guns to get me. You didn't come in with anything. You got guts in my book."

With that he pushed open the door and was gone. He was right. I hadn't come in with anything. Who could have guessed it would be enough?

That night I slept on the couch. I didn't have any idea how to make things right with Sandy. I couldn't dare ask to sleep in our bed, and I really was not sure I wanted to sleep in it after she left tomorrow following the funeral.

At eleven o'clock the next morning I returned to the funeral home. People milled about through the various rooms or talked in little groups. I surveyed the crowd, trying to spot Zeke, but I didn't see him. I saw two or three of the Westwood Christian Church elders, but they turned away when they saw me looking in their direction. The town was rallying around the tragedy, and I understood that. But coupled with my other problems, I felt more and more isolated and alone. I had no one to turn to or talk with about it all, not even Connie.

Connie and Billy came in a few minutes before the service started. The crowd murmured and then grew silent as Billy solemnly led a weary-looking Connie to a seat in the front row. His expression was stony, and he only nodded politely at some of the folks. While I waited to begin, I noticed his hands trembling in his lap. Connie reached over and covered them with her own hands.

That simple gesture revealed to me the power of my transgression, the ugliness of my violation of an ultimate trust.

The force of the realization rocked me back on my heels like a blow to the chest.

Connie, wounded and hurt, sheltered Billy's weakness and helplessness with her own. I had sworn before the powers of the church and the powers of the universe to do the same, not only in my marriage to Sandy, but in my union across the ages with those ordained before me. It wasn't for my father— or at least not for him alone—that I was here. I was here because I had to be. I needed to be here at this moment, wedded with these people to a most human endeavor, yet together with them seeking holy ground, even perhaps showing it to them.

The room swam before my eyes. The revelation came and went in the blink of an eye, yet the force of it reverberated through every cell in my body, in every thought and feeling of my heart and soul.

"Psst, Preacher!"

The sound came to me through a tunnel. I turned and saw old Silas Mitchell gesturing for me to get the show on the road. I opened my mouth but nothing came out. My heart filled with an intense desire to tell Sandy about what had just happened. I wanted to tell her that I was a hopeless idiot, that I had been blind to something right there in front of me this whole time.

I searched the crowd. Sandy fidgeted in the last row, her thick red hair pulled back in a braid. I longed to go back and untie it and let it flow over her shoulders. How could I be so stupid, I chided myself.

"Ahem, and now, the Reverend Scott Daniels will conduct the services."

Silas firmly grasped my elbow and practically shoved me toward the podium set in front of the casket.

I stumbled and mumbled my way through the Twenty-third Psalm and the Lord's Prayer. Then it was time to talk about why we were gathered. I hoped and prayed for a surge of inspiration, for another flash of insight and strength. However, all I felt was the same old me.

Mikey Simpson was five years old, a child, when he . . . died. Jesus said, "Truly I say to you, unless you turn and become like children, you will never enter the kingdom of heaven. Whoever humbles himself like this child, he is the greatest in the kingdom of heaven."

I wonder about those words. In God's eyes it is children who have the right idea about what it means to walk with God and to live with God.

Maybe it's because children don't worry too much about getting into heaven. They are willing to trust. Children are willing to believe. They are willing to believe in things like adventure stories and faraway kingdoms with kind and good kings. They can believe that good will always overcome evil. They accept the mysteries of life as being just that, mysteries. Full of wonder and awe, children don't try to tear them apart and examine them under a microscope piece by piece.

Children, like Mikey, are more open and receptive to believing, and more importantly, to trusting. These things are what make for a meaningful life.

I heard myself saying the words, and I found myself listening eagerly, as though they came from someone else.

Mikey's life was short, but it was a full life in that he was able to know pleasure and to give pleasure. He was able to receive love and to give love. We must not look for meaning in his death, but rather we need to recognize the meaning in his life.

Consider the fact that children don't have to stop and think about being a child, or thinking like a child, or doing things they like to do. They just do it. This is fun, they say. This is an adventure. I feel good. Let's live.

Maybe that is closer to the reality of faith than all of our adult worrying about having enough of everything: enough happiness, enough pleasure, enough security. God offers a gift of faith, and love, and life. And we are to reach out and take it. And it will be ours. It will be enough. Faith, love, life—they are enough. I believe Mikey knows that to be true, even now.

At the end of the service I walked to the office of the funeral director to wait for the procession to get organized. To my surprise, Silas ushered Connie and Billy into the same room and closed the door. An awkward silence followed.

From beyond the closed doors came the sounds of the mourners filing past the casket for their final farewells. Cries of grief, whimpers of pain, even their stage whispers reached us from the other room, while our own silence stretched on.

Finally Connie spoke. "I can't do this Billy. Please help me. I can't say goodbye to my baby."

Billy said gruffly, "We have to, Honey. He needs us now. I can't fail him again."

I remained silent.

Connie turned to me and said, "I wanted you to know, Scott, that we're back together now. Billy has moved back into the house, and we've left Mikey's room just the way it was. I put his favorite little bear in his bed. Billy and I go into his room at night and sit and talk to him. We tell him how sorry we are, and not to be scared."

The door opened and Silas led us back in to the viewing room. Connie took a camera from her purse and handed it to Billy. At the casket, she carefully arranged the flowers and family pictures that were to go with Mikey to his grave. Then she bent over and kissed him on the lips. As she did, Billy snapped a picture. The flash left blue spots in front of my eyes.

Billy handed the camera to Connie, and she photographed his last kiss for his son. Billy rested his forehead on Mikey's cheek for a moment, then straightened up and walked past me without saying a word. For a long time Connie stayed by Mikey's head, stroking his hair and whispering to him, "Don't be afraid. Mommy is here. We love you. Don't be afraid in the dark."

Finally the pallbearers had to pull her away so the body could be buried. It was only then that I realized Zeke had never showed.

EIGHTEEN

It was still raining when my father arrived at Camp Fairfield to take me home. I sat on the front porch of the camp infirmary wrapped in a blanket, shivering in the chilly mountain air and from the anticipation of my father's reaction to this unexpected journey. I kept my eyes glued to the front gate and the quarter mile of dirt lane that led from the main road up to the camp. I knew he wouldn't be happy, but it would be better than staying in this alien place.

Once, while I waited, I thought I saw Sheree across the recreation field, her long hair streaming behind her as she ran to catch up with friends. The director announced over the public address system that there would be a mud bowl olympics an hour after lunch, with puddle races, splash jumps, and various other fun filled events for all campers. It sounded like it might be a lot of fun. I envisioned Sheree loping across the field toward me, a warm smile on her face as she waved to me to wait for her.

I groaned at the image, and for a brief moment I considered dashing across the rain-soaked ground to find her and tell her about what had happened last night after I had been so hurt by her deserting me on the way to the carnival. Instead, the rhythm of the camp continued unabated, and I sat shivering.

The director, the Reverend Philip Thomas Abernathy, who insisted we call him Phil, gave me a stern lecture after retrieving me from the chapel. First he chased away the curious onlookers before marching me into his paneled office decorated with moth-eaten animal pelts.

"Camper, do you know what you put us through last night?" he began, his face growing red as he paced in front of me. "Someone could have been hurt while searching the woods, and then our insurance carrier would have come down on us like a ton of bricks. The camp board goes to a lot of trouble to make this a good, Christian place for boys and girls, and your irresponsible actions could have jeopardized the whole program."

Phil rubbed his bald head and let out an exasperated sigh. "I don't know what got into you, Camper. Your cabinmates say that they've tried to make you feel at home and include you in all their activities, but that you insist on staying off by yourself and don't join in. What more can we do if you don't want to cooperate and meet them halfway, Camper?"

I figured it was best to keep my mouth shut. I spied all my gear piled in a corner, my heart sinking as I noticed my Bible tossed carelessly on a pile of firewood. Its pages were all ruffled and fluted like an accordion. Apparently one of my helpful and concerned cabinmates had tossed it into a puddle during the night.

"Are you listening to me, Camper?" Phil caught the direction of my gaze and continued in a triumphant tone. "That's right, I've called your father. Not only have you shamed Camp Fairfield, but now you have to explain your actions to him and the good people of your church that paid to send you here."

I steeled myself as I saw the old gray station wagon with the front bumper held on with a bent coat hanger turning into the dirt lane. My father stared straight ahead through the windshield. I started to wave, then changed my mind. He got out of the car and simply said, "Get your stuff, Son, while I sign you out."

I dutifully loaded the car and got into the front seat. Usually it was a pleasurable experience to get to ride up front, but I just wanted this ride to be over quickly. As we drove out the front gate I glanced back, foolishly hoping for one last glimpse of Sheree.

"Was she nice?" asked Dad.

I looked at him, surprised and suspicious. "Who?"

He laughed. "After Philip called I got another call from

a young lady named Sheree. She was quite concerned about you. She told me about last night and speculated as to what happened after you left her on the way to the carnival."

I stared, half angry and half overjoyed to hear how much she cared. "Nothing happened. I don't want to talk about it."

"Okay," he said.

"And besides, I didn't leave her, she left me," I added defiantly.

"That reminds me," Dad said in his tone of voice that I recognized from all the sermons I had listened to over the years. "Since you don't want to talk about it, how about if I tell you about what I've been working on for this week's sermon? It will help me to think it through out loud and pass the time while I drive. Okay?"

I shrugged. Who cares about me, I pouted. I've just come through the worst night of my life and he's going to give me a sermon.

"It's about the story of the prodigal son. You know me, I can't resist a good story. Anyway, I got to thinking, we always talk about the father and how he viewed his sons. But what about the two boys? How did they view their father? Interesting, wouldn't you say?"

About as interesting as athlete's foot, I groused to myself, ignoring him and watching the shops of Ligonier go past as we turned onto Route 30 for the trip back to Pittsburgh.

He continued, undaunted. "Take the younger son, the one who runs away. He probably saw his father as oppressive, overly demanding, too restrictive. He had a passion to find out for himself about life and love. He goes off and makes mistakes, big ones, and he tests the limits of love, and he finds out there is a huge cost attached to the kind of love his father shows.

"Now the older one, the one who stays, he's afraid of passion. He's afraid to break the rules. Dad is a stickler for rules, according to this son. Dad's a hopeless old fool, and this boy is going to bide his time until he gets what he wants. Which is all well and good, but he misses out on love. He doesn't want to pay the price, so he misses out. What do you think?"

I shrugged again. My dad's voice softened and he sounded almost wistful, as though he had forgotten I was there in the car with him.

"I wish I could go all out like the prodigal son and explore that kind of love. It must be something else."

He sighed and looked over at me. "Do you understand what I mean?"

But I didn't answer. I didn't understand, not until after what happened many years later following Mikey Simpson's funeral.

NINETEEN

The present time
"You ever dance, Preacher Boy?"

I swear Zeke could materialize out of thin air. I had parked my car along River Road and perched on the rocks above the paper mill spillway. The treated sewage emptied into the river to begin its journey through the innumerable water systems of the towns downstream. I watched Zeke come closer, singing "Old Dan's Records" as he stumbled over the boulders and discarded tires that littered the bank. He didn't act surprised to see me, so I figured he had been looking for me.

"Have I ever danced, is that what you said, Zeke?" This day was not a day for dancing or singing. Mikey lay in the ground, my house sat empty even with me in it, and this old drunken fool wanted to talk about dancing.

"Yeah, dancing. Have you ever danced? I bet you ain't, am I right? Your heart and brain are strangers to each other, so I can't imagine your feet just up and carrying you off in a dance." The late afternoon sun turned the water in the river deep green, and the shadows on the hills grew longer and softer, while I contemplated Zeke's analysis.

"You're right, Zeke. I don't dance, and I didn't know you were a Gordon Lightfoot fan." My brain and emotions were too exhausted to spar with him.

Zeke laughed. "I like good music, Preacher Boy, and I certainly need some good music to get through today." He settled on a rock and studied me "I hear you gave a real nice funeral for Mikey. Thanks."

We sat in silence, watching the water's constant plunge over the concrete dam, the gurgling, muted roar sounding an antiphonal note to the doleful and grim reality I faced.

"I don't feel much like dancing, Zeke, even if I could.

After the funeral Sandy packed up and took the kids to Pittsburgh."

"I know," he said, sobering up for the moment. "I'm sorry to hear it. What are you going to do?"

I picked up a pebble and threw it at the river. "I don't know. Seems like I've screwed up big time, and I don't have a clue as to what to do next."

Zeke jumped up. "I do," he shouted, and proceeded to stick his left foot into the air and start singing, "You put your left foot in, you put your left foot out; you do the hokey pokey and you shake it all around. That's what it's all about."

I shook my head in utter disbelief, looking around to see if anyone was watching.

"Come on," yelled Zeke, pulling at my arm.

I pushed him away, and he abruptly sat down.

"Mikey called me Grunk," he said. "Don't that beat all? Grunk. I never could figure out where he got that name. I guess it was his version of Grandpa Zeke."

I laughed until I thought of Sammy and Brandy going off to live with Grandma and Grandpa Wertz. "My kids call my father-in-law Granpoohpa."

"What about your dad? What do they call him?" Zeke asked.

"He, uh, they don't call him anything. My father is dead and has been for a long time. My kids didn't know him and never will."

"They know you, don't they?" Zeke's good eye bored into me.

"What's that supposed to mean?" I asked warily.

"You ended up with the calling, didn't you? Well, it had to have fertile ground to take root in you. Your daddy did what he could to prepare you for the calling, and now you do the same for your kids. He gave you a big part of himself so you would know the calling when it came."

"He didn't give me any part of himself, Zeke," I scoffed. "He gave everything to the church and to my mom. There wasn't anything left for me."

"He showed you the light, didn't he? Sometimes that's all you can do for people, give yourself away completely with no chance of knowing if the light got through or not. But you got to keep trying, letting the light get through."

"Zeke, the light's gone out of me," I said flatly.

"I don't believe that, Preacher Boy."

"It's true. I quit, I'm through, I'm out of here after this festival tonight."

"So Sonny runs you out of town, and you leave him here to poison this church. Listen, Preacher Boy, I knew about you and Connie. I'm not stupid. I knew you were searching for something and you thought she might have the answer."

My mouth dropped open and I squirmed on the rock, feeling exposed in front of this unlikely prophet.

"So what are you going to do about it?" I asked him. "What do you want from me?"

He laughed until that awful cough hit him with a violent attack. When he could continue, Zeke gasped, "I don't want anything, don't fret yourself." He leaned forward until the wheezing abated. "Whew, that was a nasty one. It must be time for a drink. Care to join me, Preacher Boy?"

"Did you ever talk to Connie about it?" I ignored his invitation.

"Nope, nor Billy either. I figured nobody made me a judge and jury. I know it isn't the answer, though, for you. I had confidence that you'd figure it out and realize that you were supposed to be getting out of the way, not getting in the way."

"You lost me, old man. Getting out of the way of what or whom?"

Zeke stood up. "Time for that drink. Time to leave the dead to bury the dead."

Why am I sitting here trying to figure out what this crazy drunk is talking about I asked myself. "What do you think I should do?"

"I think you should learn how to dance, Preacher Boy.

It would come in real handy for weddings and funerals." With that, he stumbled off toward Fat Eddie's.

That evening the street in front of the church was closed off at both ends. The festival was a big event in the small community, a chance to let loose for a few hours of entertainment and excitement. Colored lights hung between the telephone poles up and down Main Street, swaying high above the crowd strolling along the thoroughfare which had been transformed into a carnival midway. Booths lined both sides of the street, and every imaginable game of chance beckoned while country music blared from the loudspeakers set up at the booth for Cumberland radio station WCTY. An endless variety of food booths filled the air with pungent odors that enticed passersby to eat themselves silly. In keeping with the theme of Old-fashioned Days, all those working the booths and selling tickets were decked out in full hoop skirts, bonnets, suspenders, sleeve rings, straw hats, high top shoes, and whatever else they could dig out of the attic.

Some in the town wondered out loud if the festival should be canceled in light of the tragic event. In fact, Sonny had obviously been counting on that when he called for the special session meeting. But word soon spread that the grief-stricken Connie called Esther Savacini, imploring her to see that it proceeded as planned. So the showdown meeting was postponed.

Mikey's death was the talk of the town, naturally, but by the time dusk arrived the street was full of laughing, bustling crowds, testing their skill, their luck, and the limits of their stomachs.

I took all this in as I gingerly came out the front doors of the church and made my way toward the dunking booth. I wore a heavy, woolen, extremely tight-fitting, old-fashioned bathing suit. The leggings covered my knees, reaching midcalf. The buttons for the top strained around my belly. The overall effect was not helped by the broad, bright green and yellow horizontal stripes. All those donuts and cookies had done their work, I noticed ruefully, and I looked like some sort of mutant squash.

Climbing up the ladder at the dunking booth for my first shift, I paused to survey the scene. Down in the valley, light from the mill colored the haze of twilight on the horizon with an orange glow. Tree-covered slopes reached toward a purple sky. At the far end of Main Street I could catch a glimpse of the river working its way through the valley before it passed out of sight under the bridge and around Last Hope Bend. The vista reminded me of Billy's abandoned dream from that grim night at the American Legion hall when I first saw his paintings. His ambiguity and sense of being trapped in a sylvan jail brought to mind my father's long ago wistful desire to be like the prodigal son and have the courage to abandon rigid expectations in search of love's reckless freedom.

Is that what God's love is like I found myself wondering. Sandy had really left me, I was alone, and I felt as though I teetered on the brink of a bottomless chasm when I stepped out onto the small board set above the tank of cold water. Sandy had really left me. I was alone.

"C'mon, Preacher, plant it so we can take a crack at you."

Some of the junior high boys from the congregation waited impatiently in the front of the line, eager for their chance at revenge for the agonies of Sunday school and confirmation class. Steeling myself for the first shock, I settled onto the narrow seat suspended over the tank.

The first half-dozen aspiring pitchers tried unsuccessfully to hit the target that stuck out to the side and was attached by a steel arm and hinge to the bench where I sat. As each of them took their three tosses for a dollar and I remained dry, the tension and excitement increased and the crowd grew more boisterous.

Some began to taunt me. "He's rigged it so he can't fall."

"Unplug your bathing suit, Preacher, before I go blind."

I laughed good-naturedly and let go of the poles on each side. The spotlight behind me cast my shadow over the water tank and onto the crowd. With my arms spread-eagled I looked like a clown on a cross, I noticed with some irony.

Suddenly the crowd grew quiet. Some backed away uneasily from the sawhorses set around the tank, nervously glancing at each other as they parted and gave way to the next player.

"Let me have a shot at him."

I froze. There, casually tossing a baseball from one hand to the other, stood Sonny. Instinctively I dropped my arms to protect my soft belly. Sonny ignored the murmurs of the onlookers for a long moment as he sized up his target.

I knew that earlier in the day the police had ruled the tragedy was an accident. There was no way Sonny could have seen or avoided the darting boy. Sonny was in the clear. But what kind of fool or idiot would show up tonight, I wondered, accident or not? I seethed at being confronted in such a ridiculous position. The embodiment of all my frustration and loathing stood there, staring me in the face.

Sonny made a great show of selecting the spot from which to throw. Then he meticulously rolled up each sleeve.

"Don't worry, Mister Daniels. It'll be over quick."

He let out a low laugh and went into a long windup.

Just as his arm came up over his head, loud screaming sounded from the far end of the midway. It was a scream of sheer terror, followed by panicky shrieks and shouts, and pandemonium ensued. The onlookers at the dunking tank began hurrying toward the sounds. Cries of "Get the police!" and "He's got a gun, watch out!" served to speed up the onrush.

Immediately I started to work my way back across the bench so I could climb down the ladder. Something was terribly wrong.

"Oh no you don't."

I looked up. Sonny still stood there, arm cocked to throw. I watched transfixed as his arm came forward. Sonny's aim was true and with a loud clang the target arm swung back, releasing the bench. For a moment nothing happened. Then in a rush I plunged into the icy water, my ears ringing with Sonny's laughter sounding above the frightened din.

When I surfaced, the first thing I saw was Sonny's back as he hurried away, in the opposite direction from the apparent scene of the trouble. I started to shout something after him, changed my mind, and tried to clamber out of the tank. It took several tries before I could finally swing one sodden leg over the edge and pull my body after it. I had no choice then but to heave myself over the top and unceremoniously flop to the ground with a squishy thump.

I jumped up and started running toward the clamor. The debris on the street cut and bruised my bare feet. At one point, near the kissing booth, I tripped, and sprawled flat, catching a face full of pavement. When I got up I could taste salty liquid flowing from my nose and across my lips. The awkward bathing suit weighed a ton and dragged me down as I tried to push my way through the crowd gathered in front of the church.

"What's going on here?" I demanded to know.

"Oh, Preacher, thank God you're here," gasped Esther Savacini, her eyes wide and wild.

"Where are the police?" someone shouted.

"What's going on?" I asked again, bewildered.

A woman dressed like a flapper from the twenties spoke up. "It's Billy Simpson. The children from the junior class were all gathered here on the church steps collecting money for the Mikey fund, when all of a sudden Billy shows up, dressed in his old army uniform, his face made up in green and brown camouflage paint."

"What?" I said incredulously.

"She's right. I saw him," confirmed a burly man. "He pulled out a pistol and started waving it around, telling everybody to get back, he was taking the kids."

The flapper picked up the story. "He herded them all together and took them in there." She gestured toward the front doors.

"Why? Does anybody know why?" I insisted.

They all shook their heads. I looked around, desperately searching for God knows what. The crowd looked at me expectantly.

"How many kids are in there?" I asked, stalling for time to think this through.

"Seven or eight."

I shuddered. Somebody had to do something. Billy had gone over the edge, and there was no telling what he might do or how much time we had until he did it. A teenage boy came running down the street and stopped in front of me, panting from the exertion.

"They can't come," he gasped. "The cops are all up at the mill. There's been some kind of accident or something. Mildred's trying to reach them on the radio."

I groaned. Nobody stepped forward with any suggestions.

"I'll go in," I said quietly. "We can't wait."

"No, it's too dangerous, Preacher. He's crazy. Wait for the authorities," said the owner of the bakery.

"I can't wait."

A part of me couldn't believe how calm I sounded. I took a deep breath. "Stand back everybody. I don't want anybody else coming in here, do you understand?"

The crowd nodded and fell back. I stood alone in my outlandish outfit. In the darkened glass I could see the reflection of steam rising from the bathing suit in the chilly night air, wreathing my head in wisps of mist. I tried to focus my thoughts and pray, but nothing happened.

Finally I gave up and stepped to the doors. I reached for the handle and slowly and quietly pulled one open. Without looking back, I slipped into the waiting darkness.

TWENTY

The stillness in the foyer unsettled me. I don't know exactly what I expected, but not this eerie peacefulness. I couldn't hear the crowd any longer, and there was no sign of Billy and the children. The silence troubled me. If Billy had left the front door totally unguarded, where would he have taken the children that would still allow him to feel secure?

I knew I had better find out, which meant I would have to sneak around in the darkened building, trying to locate them without setting off any alarms in Billy's mind that he was under attack. This seemed a fairly unlikely scenario considering my lack of coordination. As if to confirm my self-critique, a picture flashed through my mind of that day in the woods when I went hunting with Billy.

"Yep, I'm in big trouble," I muttered under my breath.

I tried to visualize the layout of the church and any obstacles I needed to avoid. Oh please, don't let him be in the furnace room, I silently pleaded. Maybe this wasn't such a good idea after all, Scott.

The sound of laughter drifted down from somewhere overhead. I held my breath, wondering if under the strain I might be hallucinating. I heard it again.

I gingerly felt my way along the wall until I touched the railing of the stairs leading up to the sanctuary. I placed the weight of one foot on the first stair, testing for any squeaks. There were none, so I tried my other foot on the next stair. Slowly I inched my way up to the landing, where the stairway turned sharply left. A few more steps and I would be at the doors to the sanctuary. After that there would be no turning back.

I decided not to wait too long on the landing. Now that I was in the church I was beginning to wonder what had possessed me to think I knew what I was doing. This was a job for the police, not Rambo Preacher. I tried to imagine the scene in the sanctuary, frightened children and a mad gunman huddled in a corner, and used that apocalyptic vision to motivate me to continue on up the steps.

As I resumed my slow journey, however, I heard the laughter again. It was not the wild shrieks of a madman but the laughter of children enjoying themselves. Throwing caution to the wind, I ran on tiptoe the rest of the way to the top. When I pressed myself against the heavy doors leading to the sanctuary, the feel of the itchy wool reminded me that I still wore the bizarre bathing suit. The realization took some more wind out of my sails, and I considered abandoning the craziness of what I was about to do.

But I couldn't. Something forced me onward, giving me the guts to peek in through the small pane of glass set in the door. My mouth dropped open. The only light in the room came from the two burning worship candles on the communion table in the front of the room. The dancing flames cast waving shadows under the cross. A group of children leaned over the table, intent on the papers in front of them, busily coloring with crayons and markers.

I squinted through the thick glass, pressing my cheek to the cool pane as I tried to look into all the corners of the darkened sanctuary. I wanted to locate Billy. I was so intent on my search that for a brief second, I ignored the cold steel pressed into the back of my neck. Then the reality dawned in a sickening rush.

"Don't move."

I could feel Billy's hot breath on my cheek as he leaned his weight against me, pinning me to the door.

"You move one inch and you're a dead man."

His hands quickly patted me down, looking for weapons. My heart clamored against my chest; I dared not breathe.

"Why are you sneaking up on these kids?" The rasp of his voice was a menacing whisper of wind in the stillness.

"Unhh . . ." My fright and his grip had immobilized everything, including my vocal cords.

The gun barrel pressed harder, till I cried out in pain.

"Billy, it's me!"

"How do you know my name, gook?"

The pressure lessened momentarily, as if he might be confused. I didn't know if that was a hopeful sign or not.

"Billy, it's me, the preacher."

"Whoever you are, you can't get to those kids. Somebody's got to protect them so none of them gets shot."

It didn't take a genius to figure it out. Burying his own son had pushed Billy over the edge. In his tortured mind he was back in Vietnam trying to keep some half-crazed teenage soldier from killing a wide-eyed child.

I wanted to laugh and cry and scream out my own insane terror. I tried to focus on my breathing, hoping to direct my careening thoughts into some course of action.

"Billy, let them go and I'll stay here with you."

An evil chuckle came from the back of his throat, and he moved the end of the barrel into my right ear.

"You'd like that, wouldn't you, gook?" His voice turned hard and cold. "I'm not stupid. You've got an ambush set up out there that'll wipe those kids out. No deal." He jerked me away from the door, opened it, and sent me through with a violent kick.

I sprawled in the aisle between the pews. The children at the communion table looked back at me and began to giggle, pointing at my funny clothes.

"Reverend Daniels," said Susie Becker, "you look funny."

"Yeah," chimed in Danny Worthington. "Is that your underwear?"

That brought on new gales of laughter. I slowly picked myself up off the floor, trying to act casual.

"We're playing a game with Mister Simpson," little Chuckie Savacini, Esther's grandson, piped up.

"Yeah," said Susie. "We're making pictures. Mister Simpson said if we want to get out of this place before we get too old we have to be artists. He'll protect us until we can take care of ourselves."

The others all nodded in unison, oblivious to the danger they were in. It made sense to me, remembering the conversation with Billy behind the American Legion hall. In his grief and pain at Mikey's death everything was getting all jumbled up: his feelings of being trapped, the failure of his marriage, and the nightmare of Vietnam that would never give him peace. I felt sorrow and compassion for the man.

"I'll see if I can help you," I said, trying to make my voice sound matter-of-fact while my mind raced a mile a minute.

"I know what you're doing," Billy muttered, low enough that only I could hear. "Don't think you can turn them against me. I'll kill you first. They got Mikey, but they won't get these kids."

My heart broke.

I heard scurrying sounds and a door closing on the ground floor. Billy quickly stepped over to the rear doors, opened one, and shouted into the darkness, "I've got your leader in here, gooks. You try to come in and I'll blow his head off!"

The scurrying noises immediately stopped. In the dim light from the candles I could see sweat on Billy's forehead. He looked me up and down and slowly smiled.

"What kind of uniform is that? You so hard up in this war that they make you wear *that*?" Some of the tension trickled out of my body. Maybe I could find a way to connect with the Billy that I knew.

"Do you ever have dreams, Billy?"

He looked at me quizzically before going back to the door to listen. When he was satisfied, he waved me to the front with the pistol.

"What kind of a question is that?" he asked.

He went up the three steps to the chancel and walked around the table, praising the children's efforts, while I asked myself the same thing.

"I don't know. It's just a question." I forced an air of nonchalance into my voice.

Billy sat down with his back to the pulpit, his eyes always moving, roving around the room, alert to any threat or attack. Finally he shrugged.

"Yeah, I have dreams. I dream I'm eating a giant marshmallow and when I wake up my pillow is gone."

The children howled at that, and Billy smiled appreciatively. I ignored it, going on instinct and adrenaline.

"What else do you dream?"

He looked at me suspiciously. In my mind I pictured police and swat teams positioning themselves around the church, searchlights being set up, sharpshooters getting into place, the crowd anxiously awaiting any word on our fate. I wondered if anyone would call Sandy. "I dream about fishing and hunting." He stroked his mustache, looking sober. "And about Mikey. I dream about Mikey."

"He was a good boy, Billy. He loved you a lot. And I know you loved him."

Billy bowed his head, the gun drooping in his hand. Suddenly he snapped back to full alert.

"Somebody has to protect these little ones." He gestured toward the young artists who watched in silence, now looking alarmed by the twists in this strange game.

"Keep going, Scott," I told myself. "Dear God, help me to keep going."

"Why does a gook like you kill my kids?" asked Billy, his eyes filling with hate.

"Billy, it's me, the preacher. I'm not here to hurt the kids. I'm here to help you and to help them."

I kept my tone of voice level and quiet. Maybe Pastoral Care and Counseling 101 would be of some use after all. Except I don't remember them dealing with hostages and over-the-edge gunmen.

"I want to go home," said little Chuckie. "And I have to go to the bathroom."

"It's too dangerous out there, ain't it, Chaplain?" Billy looked uncertain.

I breathed easier. At least now I was the chaplain instead of the enemy. Hang in there, I silently pleaded. Hang in there, Billy. We'll get you home.

"I can see that they're safe, Billy. I think their parents would like to know that they're safe and maybe I could take them out of here so their moms and dads can take care of them for you." I studied his face, looking for a sign of a break-through. "You want them to be safe, don't you?"

"I don't know, Chaplain. Mikey was with his mommy and look what happened. I should have been there. I should have been protecting him. Now somebody shot him dead. It was dark, you understand? It was dark, and they said to go in and clean out the village. I was scared, totally scared. It was a sound, just a sound, but I fired at it. Now Mikey's gone. His eyes, Preacher, his eyes, they tore me up. Oh God, now Mikey's gone." Billy buried his face in his hands, totally despondent in his confused grief.

I motioned to the kids to come down and sit in the pew behind me. They silently obeyed, staring in awe at Billy as they filed past. I knew that I was incredibly fortunate to get this far, and I prayed for wisdom on how to proceed.

"Billy," I said gently.

He looked up, his face a mask of despair and sorrow.

"Billy, it's time for the kids to go home."

He nodded. I told Susie to lead the children down the stairs after I turned on the lights for them. Before they could begin moving toward the rear, little Chuckie ran back to the communion table and picked up his picture. Going over to the forlorn figure, the boy laid it over the gun in Billy's lap.

"Here, Mister Simpson, it's for you. It's a picture of the mountains and the river and the bridge. I thought you might like to keep it since your little boy can't make you pictures any more."

He skipped down the stairs to rejoin the line. At the door I went first to turn on the lights. As the children filed past, I called down the stairs, "Here come the children. Everyone is safe and sound."

"Aren't you coming?" called an authoritative voice from below.

"No, I'm going to talk to Billy some more. I'll be fine."

"Scott, it's me, Connie." She sounded tired and frightened. "I want to come up and talk to Billy."

I could hear several voices talking together, then Connie's high pitched protests.

"No, he needs me. I'm going to him."

"Connie!" I yelled.

The babble of voices stopped.

"Please be patient, Connie. I don't think it's a good idea to let anyone else come in right now. I'll tell Billy, though, that you want to see him."

With that I went back inside, not wanting to leave Billy alone for too long. He still sat in front of the pulpit, rubbing his cheek with the barrel of the gun. I sat in the front pew again, acutely aware of the cross, eerily lit by the candles, rising above us both, wreathed by dancing tendrils.

"You're an idiot, Preacher."

"I could have told you that, Billy."

He laughed. "Why didn't you keep on going?"

"Somebody's got to make sure the candle wax doesn't get on the carpet. Esther Savacini would just die if anything happened to our precious carpeting."

"You're crazier than I am, Preacher."

"Maybe so, Billy."

A stray breeze stirred the flames on the candles as we sat in silence. I marveled at the strange calmness that had settled over me at some point since entering the sanctuary in that flying heap. I decided to let go and allow that serenity lead me.

"I can't take the pain any more, Preacher." Billy leaned his head back against the light wood of the pulpit, the gun on the floor beside him.

"It must be very hard for you," I offered, "to believe in a God who would let so much pain happen."

"That's the funny thing," said Billy. "I don't have trouble believing in God. I have trouble believing in me. I look at Zeke and I wonder if that's me in a few more years. I look at Connie and I ask why anyone like her would love me. She's so good to me and I'm a complete jerk to her. I don't get it, Preacher, do you?"

Hearing Billy mention Connie jabbed at my newfound strength. Maybe I didn't get it either. Who was I to tell Billy anything, anything about living, about trusting God, about loving a woman, about believing?

"I've watched you, Billy. I've watched you care about Joey McCrady, I've watched you care about Mikey and care about me. Loving somebody else, even God, isn't about finding yourself. It's about losing yourself. Love is giving yourself away. I can remember my dad saying he wished he could find it, and I've seen you do it. That's an awful lot to have going for you in my book."

Billy didn't say anything.

I leaned forward, feeling my heart jump to my throat as I asked, "Can I have the gun, Billy?"

"You must be wanting to go home, Preacher. Sandy's probably worried sick about you."

I started to reply, to tell him that Sandy was gone. Then I stopped. What purpose would it serve at the moment?

Noticing my hesitation, Billy picked up the gun and handed it to me.

"Go on," he said. "Go home. You've earned it. I'm sorry if I scared you."

I took the gun gingerly, holding it by the barrel. "I don't know what will happen next, Billy. There are police outside, and Connie. I'll tell them what happened."

"It's okay, Preacher. Everything will be okay."

Billy stood up and shook my hand. Then he went to the communion table and stared up at the cross, the picture from Chuckie lay on the wood in front of him. At the door I turned around for a last look. He still stood there, silently lost in the protective shadow.

"It's me, Reverend Daniels," I called down as I descended the stairs.

Policemen swarmed around me as I reached the bottom and handed over the gun.

"Where is he?" they demanded impatiently.

"He's up there," I pointed. "He's okay, take it easy. I brought down the gun."

"You fool," said one officer. "He's an ex-Ranger. He wouldn't have gone into what he thought was a combat situation without more than one weapon."

"No," I protested. "It's okay. I think he's pray—"

A loud blast shattered the night. The gunshot echoed in the now empty sanctuary. I froze as uniforms frantically streamed past me up the stairs. In a daze I wandered outside, pulling at the outlandish costume I still wore. Struggling to breathe, I walked through the crowd of police cars and fire trucks drawn up around the church.

At the bridge I sat down and wept, stunned and empty.

TWENTY-ONE

"Likewise the Spirit helps us in our weakness; for we do not know how to pray as we ought, but the Spirit himself intercedes for us with sighs too deep for words."

There it was, my dad's prayer—his personal paraphrase of Romans 8:26—from all those years ago, beyond words, beyond memories, beyond self. I figured I had no chance to sleep, the house being too empty without Sandy and the kids, and besides, I kept hearing that gunshot over and over every time I closed my eyes.

I wandered down to the basement and dug out my old briefcase from seminary. There lay the old, musty Bible, the pages of the sermon from that fateful day still marking the nexus of mine and my father's journey. I wasn't interested in the sermon this time, but rather my father's words on the back of the yellowing pages: "for son—my prayer," and the reference from Romans 8.

I carried it back upstairs and sat in the light of the moon streaming through the windows, staring at my memories and my follies, rereading the phrase "the Spirit himself intercedes for us with sighs too deep for words." Billy's fate had taken me to a place too deep for words, I knew that to be true. I had not seen Zeke since Billy . . .

I couldn't finish the thought. It was as though Zeke had vanished into thin air, or in a puff of blue smoke from the barrel of the .9mm "assassin's special" that Billy had hidden in the pulpit Bible. I had not slept in the forty-eight hours since the paramedics tried to stem the flow of Billy's blood as it stained the wood of the communion table and dripped onto a child's simple picture of mountains and a river.

Later that afternoon Esther called to say the ladies of the church could not get the bloodstains out of the letters carved into the front edge of the sacramental table—"In remembrance of me." I told her to leave them there.

Nothing had changed. Nothing but me.

There was no word from Sandy, and I did not try to call her. I knew I needed to face the music, something I have never been good at doing. I wanted to crawl into her lap and ask her to forgive me, to face me straight on, to see everything that I was and wanted to be. But the inevitability of my falling short took my courage away.

I killed my dad. I killed Billy. The play of moonlight on Sandy's plants gave me a sensation, faint but certain, of a great loss that emptied me, leaving me grasping for belief and reassurance.

Then it struck me. I loved them. I loved them both, my dad and Billy, and I wanted to tell them that. I wanted so desperately to tell them. A nightingale's song floated on the breeze through the open window and I cried. I cried until I slept with no dreams.

"The session has taken a vote," intoned Sonny. "We no longer have confidence in your leadership, Mister Daniels. We realize that your life is in a turmoil at the moment, but still we feel that for the good of Westwood Christian Church and the good people who depend upon it for spiritual sustenance, that you need to resign so we can find someone better suited to our congregation's needs."

I felt relieved.

"Some in the congregation want a chance to take a vote, too," piped up Esther Savacini. She cast a sidelong look at Sonny as she added, "You can preach for the last time this Sunday, and then the trustees have a special announcement to make about the bright financial future for our church."

"Don't be so hasty, Esther," said a red-faced Sonny. "I'm not about to let this travesty of my mother's deathbed change in her will go unchallenged, you can bet on that. I'll see this church in court."

No, nothing has changed, I thought. Nothing but me. I

stood and walked out, wondering what to say to the congregation on Sunday.

Sunday morning I left the empty house for the final journey down Horse Rock. After worship I planned to drive to Pittsburgh, find Sandy, and tell her I had to have her back in my life, that things would change, starting with me. First, though, on the way I planned a stop at Memorial Hospital to see Andrea Orr one last time. I owed her that much.

As worship began, my mind was a blank. When I stood to speak, it seemed inevitable to choose Romans 8. "Likewise the Spirit helps us in our weakness . . ." I began and stopped. I knew I was an empty vessel, ready for intercession on a level deeper than words. What could I say, though? All I had to offer was weakness.

The crowd stirred a bit as my silence stretched on for minutes. Then a strange thing happened. The doors at the back of the sanctuary opened. In walked Zeke holding a calico kitten. He walked down the center aisle, stopped halfway to the front, and turned to address the people.

"This is Halfpenny," he said proudly, holding the wide-eyed kitten high in the air. "She is a new beginning for me. And I want to thank the preacher for making that beginning possible."

He turned to look at me. "Reverend Daniels, you're a good man. I want you to know that. I believe in you. You're no preacher boy, and I'm sorry if I insulted you. You're a man of God, and it's a shame these hard-hearted fools don't want to see that."

He walked up to the communion table and set Halfpenny on it. Softly he stroked the wood, his back to the congregation, speaking as if to himself.

"This is my son's blood here."

He traced the carved letters of "remembrance" with a gnarled finger, caressing the darkened "m-e-m" where Billy's blood made an indelible mark.

"Thank you, Scott," he said simply, looking at me, his

eyes brimming. "Thank you for caring about my son. God will show you the way."

With that, he shambled back down the aisle, coughing and wheezing. At the doors he turned back and shouted to me,

"Hey, I almost forgot. Scott, there's a young lady waiting at the Holiday Inn in Cumberland for you."

The people gasped, some shaking their heads in disgust. Sonny Orr jumped to his feet while motioning to the ushers to get rid of the bum.

"I hope you don't mind," continued Zeke, enjoying the fuss, "but I called Sandy in Pittsburgh and told her of a match made in heaven. She's eager to see you, Reverend Daniels. You'll know what to do."

He pushed open the doors, cooing to Halfpenny as he headed for Fat Eddie's. My farewell sermon forgotten, I ran out the back and jumped into my car. Halfway to Cumberland I remembered Andrea Orr. The old struggle immediately tore at me. But I knew what I had to do.

At the hospital I paced in the lobby remembering Sonny's threats. Then it struck me: Zeke had not called me preacher boy during his remarkable performance. I laughed out loud until the volunteer at the information desk asked if I needed help.

Having taken the elevator to Andrea's floor, I slowly made my way down the hall of the hospice wing. The door to her room was partially closed. I hesitated, then gently pushed on it. It was a private room, furnished with lush carpeting, walls covered with expensive wallpaper in a subdued pattern, a bureau of dark wood, and a comfortable easy chair that occupied one corner. The bed, however, was unmistakably a hospital bed.

I saw all this in a glance. It was the odor that stopped me in my tracks. It was awful, a nauseating combination of bodily waste, antiseptic, and the all-prevailing stench of decaying flesh.

The fetid smell came from the bed. I tried to breath

through my mouth as I gingerly stepped closer and looked down. I barely recognized the skeletal form of Andrea. She had been hideously aged by the pain, wasting away in its torturous grip. Little flesh remained on her frame. Her lips were drawn back away from her teeth in a gruesome death mask. Her breathing was labored and noisy, her eyes closed.

I tried to picture her in her bedroom at home, celebrating life and communion on a stormy summer afternoon. I pulled a chair over to the bed, sat down, and took her hand in mine. It was feather light, the veins knobby blue cords, the translucent skin cold to my touch.

"Mrs. Orr," I spoke softly, uncertain if she could hear me. "Andrea?"

The fragile hand tightened ever so slightly in mine.

"Andrea, it's me, Scott. Scott Daniels."

Her hand moved again.

"Do you remember me? Do you know who I am?"

It was a question I had asked myself enough times in these past two days.

There was a faint groan as she nodded her head, her eyes still closed. The nurses at the station told me she was close to slipping into a final coma. At the moment, though, she was still here. I saw tears begin to trickle from the corner of one eye and run across the crevices in her cheek.

I noticed that her lips were dry and cracked. On the bed stand I saw a plastic cup holding glycerine swabs. I picked one up and wet her lips with it. Then I sat and watched for a moment, shock and grief overwhelming my own self-doubts. I thought of Zeke's question when we were out on the trestle in the dark night, about the suffering of the innocent. Then I remembered his words about peace, purpose, and place. None of that offered adequate comfort in this living hell.

I began to lose my nerve, wondering what I was doing here, all alone, bleeding from my own wounds. Finally I took out my pocket Bible and thumbed its pages trying to reach the Twenty-third Psalm. I still held on to Andrea's fragile hand, not willing to break the connection, while I awkwardly searched for the right page. When I found it I quietly read the promising words of help from beyond our limits.

When I finished, I closed the book and in a hushed voice I began to repeat the Lord's Prayer: "Our Father, who art in heaven, hallowed be thy name . . ."

Heart-wrenching moans interrupted me, until I realized they came from Andrea. I stopped for a moment, puzzled, and then it dawned on me that she was trying to recite the prayer along with me. A holy vortex swirled around us both as I continued to pray to the soul-baring accompaniment of her ghastly lamentation.

When I finished the prayer, I couldn't think of anything further to do and stood up.

"Andrea," I said, leaning close over the bed, "I've got to go now. I'll be back as soon as I can."

The hollowness of my promise hit me as hard as the smell of decay. I backed away uncertainly from the bed, my duty complete.

"Sonny?"

Her eyes sprang open. I froze.

"Sonny?" She said it again, clearly, and I staggered as I backed into the door jamb.

"No, Andrea, it's me, Scott. Remember?" I put a light touch into my voice, belying my quaking knees. What was happening? I wanted to get out of there.

"Sooonnnyyy!" The cry was filled with anguish, her mouth gaping open, showing gray and purple. Her cheeks glistened with tears, and sweat stood out on her brow.

I hesitated, my mind a confusion of tumbling thoughts and feelings. Further attempts to clarify who I was would be futile, I divined, but I wanted her to know that it was me, not Sonny. No, certainly not Sonny at her side.

Caught in this devil's turn, I could not bear to stay; I could not bear to leave. My hands shook as I reached for the door, gulping for air. I raised my face to the ceiling, looking for an angel of mercy to relieve me. A stillness settled over the room, and in the stillness I sensed my own question being cast back to me. "Do you know who I am?"

I returned to the bedside.

Leaning over Andrea, I reached out my hand to smooth the brittle hair back from her forehead. My other hand found hers on the sheet and tenderly stroked it.

"Sonny?"

I felt a giant rending in my chest, a dawning of light in a darkened corner of my heart. I leaned closer, my face a foot above hers. For a long moment I studied her face.

"Yes," I spoke. "Yes, Mother, I'm here."

"Don't leave me," she cried. "Please, Sonny, don't leave me now."

The day stretched into forever as I stayed there, hunched over her vulnerable form. Occasionally I touched her, held her hand, wiped her forehead, and moistened her lips.

Her life continued to slip away before my eyes. No one came in. I began to frantically search for what to say.

"Please, God, some wisdom," I begged. "How about it? I don't have a prayer."

Suddenly, a great spasm of pain racked her body. She arched her back, gasping in the horror of her own suffering. I stared, transfixed and helpless.

The spasm passed and her body quieted. I knew I had to give in. I carefully put my arms around her thin shoulders, exerting just enough pressure for her to feel the embrace. One knee on the bed, I slowly lowered my face till it was next to hers on the pillow. I put my lips close to her ear.

"Mom," I whispered, my voice shaking. "Mother . . . I love you."

I kissed her on the cheek, still holding her in the tenderest embrace.

"Oh, Sonny!" Her cry was a joyous whisper, and her lips struggled to form the words. "Oh, my Sonny. I love you too. Mommy loves you too."

Unaware of having walked back to my car, I sat in the

parking lot, blindly letting time slip past. As though waking from a dream, I realized my vision was blurry, like eyes unfocused through tears.

Gradually it dawned on me. They were not tears. My spirit was too overpowered to cry. It was a gentle, healing rain, spattering against the windshield, through which I could see the green sign for the Holiday Inn on the next hill.

A door that slammed shut so long ago in a chapel at camp slowly began to swing open as the rain softly kissed the earth, and I whispered a blessing for Andrea, for Billy, for Sonny, for all of us who share in the holy mystery of life, and for all of us who hunger for love . . . with sighs too deep for words.

About the Author

John Thomas Tuft served successfully as a pastor until a serious car accident and the series of operations that followed debilitated him, forcing him to give up his pastorate. He is currently a full-time writer with a regular column in his local newspaper and several book projects underway. He has published an inspirational book entitled *Mark My Words* which is being distributed by The Upper Room and other ministries.

John is married and has three children. He and his family make their home in Western Pennsylvania.